W9-BUD-465

THIS SIDE OF HOME

ALSO BY RENÉE WATSON

What Momma Left Me

THIS SIDE OF HOME

RENÉE WATSON

BLOOMSBURY
NEW YORK LONDON NEW DELHI SYDNEY

First published in the United States of America in February 2015
by Bloomsbury Children's Books
www.bloomsbury.com

Library of Congress Cataloging-in-Publication Data
Watson, Renée.
This side of home / by Renée Watson.
pages cm
Summary: Twins Nikki and Maya Younger always agreed on most things, but as they head into their senior year they react differently to the gentrification of their Portland, Oregon, neighborhood and the new—white—family that moves in after their best friend and her mother are evicted.
ISBN 978-1-59990-668-3 (hardcover) • ISBN 978-1-61963-213-4 (e-book)
[1. Twins—Fiction. 2. Sisters—Fiction. 3. Best friends—Fiction. 4. Friendship—Fiction. 5. Neighborhoods—Fiction. 6. Urban renewal—Fiction. 7. Dating (Social customs)—Fiction. 8. Portland (Ore.)—Fiction.] I. Title.
PZ7.W32868Thi 2015 [Fic]—dc23 2014013743

Book design by Amanda Bartlett
Typeset by Westchester Book Composition
Printed and bound in the U.S.A. by Thomson-Shore Inc., Dexter, Michigan
2 4 6 8 10 9 7 5 3 1

For Linda Christensen
my teacher, mentor, and friend

THIS SIDE OF HOME

SUMMER

CHAPTER 1

June.

The season is changing.

Portland's rain is stubborn. It shares the sky with summer's sun, refusing to leave, refusing to let the flowers breathe. But summer is determined. Her sun pushes through the cracks of the clouds, making room for her light.

By July, the sun will win. And in August we will ask her to go easy on us. We will sweat and suck Popsicles, sleep under fans, and swear this is the hottest summer ever. Even though we said that last year.

But now we are going back and forth, umbrella up, umbrella down, jacket on, jacket off. Some days there is sunshine and rain at the same exact moment.

The season is changing.

And every time the season changes from spring to summer adults start saying, "Be careful out there," because they know that summer can bring shootings and chaos with her. And when violence comes no one says, "This isn't supposed to happen here," as if this is a place where we should be accustomed to tragedy.

Every summer the media come to my neighborhood, and every fall they come to my school. Never for good.

But there *is* something good to see here.

And not just all the new pretty houses and shops that line Jackson Avenue now. There is something good here. And not just because more white families have moved to this side of town.

There's always been something good here. People just have to open their minds to see it.

CHAPTER 2

This is the way it is.

Nikki and I are identical twins, and our best friend is Essence. Mom says it's like she has triplets the way the three of us do everything together, the way we'd do anything for one another. And she's right. Essence is more like a sister than a friend, so when she stops at my locker after school and whispers to me, "We're moving," I get a sick feeling in my stomach.

"The landlord is selling the house," she says. Casual. Like what she's saying is no big deal. Like she hasn't lived directly across the street from me and Nikki our whole lives. Like we never sat on her porch swing on summer nights swinging away to imaginary places. Like she never tiptoes across the asphalt in the middle of the night to come to my house so she can escape her drunk mother.

"He said he's tired of renting," Essence says. This time not as casual as before, as if this is the first time she's realized that just because her posters have been hanging on her bedroom wall all these years doesn't mean those walls belong to her.

She owns nothing. Not even those hand-me-down blues records singing in her eyes.

"Where will you go?" I ask.

"Gresham probably, or maybe North Portland. We don't know yet."

Both places are far—at least forty-five minutes away by bus. Too far for best friends who've had to take only ten steps to get to each other their entire lives.

"Don't look at me like that," Essence says. This is her way of telling me she is about to cry, and Essence hates to cry.

I look away, pretend I'm okay.

CHAPTER 3

Getting bad news is not the way I wanted to start off my summer vacation.

It's the last day of our junior year of high school. We are officially seniors. Next year, when I come back, I'll be student body president. The results were posted this morning. I have a lot of ideas about what I want to see change at Richmond, but for now, all I am thinking about is summer vacation and enjoying every minute of it with Essence. We wait at my locker for Nikki and the boys to show up.

Devin.

Ronnie.

Malachi.

Devin, Ronnie, and Malachi are in my dad's mentorship program. In the fifth grade when we became friends, we had no idea the boys would end up the finest guys in our high school. Once they get to my locker, Essence is all smiles because now her arms are wrapped around Malachi. Essence and Malachi have been together since freshman year. They are the only couple at Richmond High who might actually know what love is. They love like spring.

Ronnie takes Nikki's hand. Their fingers intertwine like knitted yarn. Ronnie is the first boy Nikki kissed, the only boy she ever cried over after a breakup, ever got back together with and loved again.

I walk next to Devin. No hand-holding or long embrace. He kisses me on my cheek, delicately, as if my face is made of hibiscus petals. I am not used to the way his lips feel against my skin. We have always had love for each other. A brother-sister friendship. But now we have more.

The six of us leave Richmond High and head home. We walk the same way every day down Jackson Avenue, making stops at one another's blocks like a city bus. Jackson Avenue looks like most of the streets in Portland: wide sidewalks with trees that hover and shade the whole block. Branches reaching out to hug you; plump houses with welcoming porches.

Every time we walk down this street, Essence says, "This is *my* street." Because Jackson is her last name. She looks at me. "You guys don't believe me, but I'm telling you, this *whole* street was named after my great-grandfather."

Essence has all kinds of stories about her family history. I know she makes them up, but it doesn't bother me. Sometimes you have to rewrite your own history.

Malachi comes to her defense. He says to me, "Look, you and Nikki aren't the only ones who have famous names." He laughs.

The story goes like this: Mom and Dad, who are both community activists, wanted us to have names that represent creativity and strength. Mom always tells us how the agreement was that Dad could choose our names if we were girls and she would choose if we were boys. If we were boys, we would have been named Medgar and Martin. But once they found out we were girls Dad decided to give us the names of our mom's favorite poets, Maya Angelou and Nikki Giovanni.

Nikki hits Malachi lightly on his shoulder. "Don't be jealous," she says.

Devin jumps in. "Malachi has a biblical name. That fits as famous, right?"

Ronnie shakes his head. "Uh, no. I mean, who remembers what Malachi did in the Bible? No one ever mentions him."

We all laugh.

As we walk down Jackson Avenue, I take in all the newness, all the change. I turn to Devin and say, "Remember that house?" I point to the pale-yellow bungalow that takes up the entire corner with its wraparound porch. It no longer has its wobbling steps, chipped paint. "I will never forget *that* day!"

"Don't remind me," Devin says, even though the memory brings a smile to his face.

We retell the story as if we don't already know.

Devin says, "That dog came out of nowhere! Just came right up to the fence growling like crazy."

I laugh. "Only I didn't know it stopped at the gate. I swear, I thought it jumped over and was chasing us."

"You took off running, Maya! Ran so fast, I could barely catch you."

And this is a big deal because Devin is an athlete and I have never been.

Then we remind each other how Ms. Thelma sat on her porch pretending to mind her business, when really she was eavesdropping and watching us to see what we were doing so she could tell our parents if we were misbehaving.

"It's so strange to see her house as a coffee shop," he says. And there is no more laughter in his voice.

For the past four years, there has been constant construction on just about every block in my neighborhood. They've painted and planted and made beauty out of decaying dreams. Block after block, strangers kept coming to Jackson Avenue, kept coming and changing and remaking and adding on to and taking away from.

About a year ago Ms. Thelma's old house became Daily Blend: Comfy. Cozy. Coffee. I wonder if those laptop-typing, free–wi-fi–using coffee drinkers know that Ms. Thelma's grandson died in that house. That a stray bullet found its home in his chest while he lay sleeping on the couch. He was only eight and only spending the night with his grandma while his parents were away to celebrate their anniversary. Wonder if they know that she had her husband's eightieth birthday celebration right there in the backyard; wonder if they know the soil used to grow Ms. Thelma's herbs and flowers and that her house always smelled good because her kitchen was full of basil, or mint, or something else fresh from her garden.

After Ms. Thelma's husband died, she moved to Seattle to live with her son, who never came to visit enough, she always said. Mom keeps in touch with her, mostly through holiday cards and phone calls on birthdays.

I wonder what Ms. Thelma would think of all these people being in her house. Wonder if she had any idea that in just four years our neighborhood would be a whole new world. And I wonder what will be different in the next four years.

Mom keeps telling me that life is only about change. Just last night she looked at me and Nikki and said, "I can't believe my little girls are all grown up now."

Nikki and I just sighed. We hate when she gets all sentimental.

"You've grown up, got your own identity and styles now," Mom said.

And this is true.

When we were kids, we spent our childhood looking just like each other, ponytails all over our heads, matching outfits with our names written on the tags so we would know what was mine, what was hers.

We have seen our reflections in each other our entire lives.

But then, freshman year, no more matching outfits. Nikki's style is made up of mismatched findings at secondhand stores and garments from the too-small-to-wear-anymore section of Mom's closet.

Sophomore year she started experimenting with color on her eyelids, lips, fingernails.

I stayed plain faced. Modest in everything except attitude, Nikki says.

Junior year, Nikki's hair had a personality all its own. Pressed straight most days, but sometimes she let it be. Natural waves swimming all over her head. My long, black strands twist like licorice and hang down my back, always braided.

All these adjustments to our outsides.

Reversible if we want to go back, be the same again. It's the changes on the inside that I'm worried about. I keep telling Mom that it feels like Nikki and I are growing apart.

She says, "There are going to be a lot of things that start changing now that you're older. You're growing up, that's all."

Maybe she is right.

Part of me is excited, but it makes me nervous, too. There are some things I like just the way they are.

CHAPTER 4

Essence's mom is a cracked vase. A woman who used to hold beauty.

I've seen pictures of Ms. Jackson and Mom when they were in high school. Mom has told me the story of how they met, of how they'd stay after school to watch the football team practice. Ms. Jackson was watching a guy named Reggie. Mom had her eyes on Dad. Mom never tells the part about how Reggie left Ms. Jackson, how when he came to the hospital two days after Essence was born he told Ms. Jackson, "This baby don't look like me," and walked out.

But Ms. Jackson tells the story all the time. Especially when she's drunk. Tonight she is pacing their living room with an empty bottle in her hand that she tries to drink from. "Got to move out of my house 'cause your trifling, no-good daddy ain't paid no child support." She stumbles over half-packed boxes, almost trips, and then yells at Essence. "Didn't I tell you to get this living room packed up? You think this stuff is going to pack itself?"

Essence finishes wrapping the plates and glasses in bubble wrap. She places them in a box, then walks over to a closet in the hallway and pulls out a dusty box that's falling apart and bursting at the seams. It has a missing flap, so it can't close properly. Essence reaches in and pulls out a stack of magazines. They are small, almost the size of thin books. "What do you want me to do with your *Jet* magazines?"

"If I got to tell you what to do, why you helping?" Ms. Jackson says. She snatches the magazines from Essence. They slip out of her hands and scatter on the floor.

I bend down and start picking them up.

"I ain't asked you to do nothing!" Ms. Jackson kneels down and picks up the magazines, cradling them in her arms in a way a mother holds her child, in a way I don't think she ever held Essence.

"Ms. Jackson, I was—I was just trying to help," I say. "Sorry."

"I don't want your sorry. And what I tell you about

calling me Ms. Jackson?" she says. "I done told you my name is Darlene."

Mom says calling adults by their first name is disrespectful. "Sorry, Ms. Darlene," I say.

She stands up, barely able to walk straight. She continues her rant, talking to me even though she isn't looking at me. She paces the living room, still nurturing her magazines. There are so many they barely fit in her arms. "Coming over here acting all siddity. You can leave and go tell your momma everything you seen here. I know that's what you gonna do. Comin' over here like a spy or somethin'—"

"Mom!" Essence says.

"You shut up and help me pack. Didn't I ask you to help me?"

Essence can't or won't look at me. I'm not sure which. She always gets this look when Ms. Jackson relapses. As if it's her fault, like she should be able to keep her mother sober. "I can't wait till I graduate so I can get away from you," Essence says.

I think Ms. Jackson might throw the magazines down and slap Essence, but instead she just yells back. "And where you think you gonna go? You hang with Maya and Nikki, but you ain't smart like them—and you don't have Mr. I-Have-a-Dream Thomas Younger as a father to pay for college."

When Ms. Jackson is drunk she calls Dad all kinds

of names. Sometimes, Mr. Thomas-Younger-Our-Next-President, or Mr. Make-the-World-a-Better-Place. I don't want to say what she calls Mom.

"I'm getting away from you," Essence says. "And I'll work my way through college if I have to. I can do hair." She holds a handful of her own braids in her hands as proof.

Ms. Jackson rolls her eyes. "You ain't gettin' into college. Not with that Richmond High education. That school ain't nothing. Not like it was when I went there. Back then we had good teachers—"

"Well, you can't tell that by looking at you!"

I wish Essence hadn't said that.

"What did you say?" Ms. Jackson asks.

I look at Essence. Hard. I shake my head.

When Essence opens her mouth, I am afraid of what might come out. She sighs and says, "Nothing, Mom. Nothing." Essence walks over to her mother. "I'm done arguing with you. Just give me the magazines so I can repack them," she says.

"I'll take care of these. You pack up that stuff." Ms. Jackson points to a bookcase that holds family pictures and a framed handprint that Essence gave her for a Mother's Day gift. We were in the third grade, and our teacher had each of us dip our hands in our favorite color of paint and make prints.

Essence walks over to the bookcase with an

empty box in hand. She dumps the picture frames in the box.

Ms. Jackson neatly packs her magazines. One by one she puts them on top of each other. "These are classics. Might be worth something one day," she says. Her voice is calm now, and I don't think she's talking to us. Or maybe she is but it doesn't matter to her if we are listening. "Do they even make *Jet* magazine anymore?" she asks. "This one here has Michael Jackson on the cover. This was back in his normal days. Back when everything was—" Ms. Jackson is still for a moment, just looking at a young Michael Jackson. She touches his face before she puts it in the box, then takes another one. "And this one—Luther. I can't throw out Luther Vandross."

Ms. Jackson talks about each magazine as she puts them in their new home. She has her own personal black history time capsule. She walks over to the sofa, dragging the box with her, and sits next to me. For each magazine, she has a story.

Essence lets out a loud sigh of boredom, of frustration. She goes upstairs. I think maybe I should go with her, but I feel like Ms. Jackson needs me to stay. She needs someone to listen to her yesterdays. She packs the last magazine, one that has the Olympic track star Flo Jo on it. "Help me tape this, please," she says.

I take the tape from the coffee table. She grabs the

scissors. Together, we close the box, store her memories once again. Before I let go of the box, Ms. Jackson grabs my hand, squeezes it tight. "Don't tell your mom, okay? Don't tell her you seen me like this," she says. "And your dad. Don't tell your dad. Promise me, okay?"

I don't answer.

"Promise me."

"Promise me you'll stop drinking," I say.

"I promise. I promise I'm gonna get myself together," Ms. Jackson says.

"I won't tell them," I say.

Ms. Jackson lets go of my hand.

We both know neither of us will keep our word.

CHAPTER 5

Essence will not tell us how she feels about moving. Instead, she curses the landlord. Rants to me and Nikki about all the things he ever did wrong.

"He never fixed the light in the bathroom; we have to hit it in order for it to come on," she says. "And the dishwasher. That thing has never worked. Not once, not ever, in seventeen years. We use it to store pots and pans." Essence takes everything out of her top dresser drawer and stuffs it into a suitcase. "He raised the rent even though he took two weeks to schedule the exterminator to come." Essence is yelling now. She slams the drawer and opens another one. "Mickey and Minnie should've been paying rent," Essence says. "Since they left Disneyland and moved in here."

Nikki can't hold back her smile. It spreads across her face and she gives in to a laugh. Essence gives in, too. Her head falls back and she laughs up to heaven, showing God her smile before the rest of us see it.

We chase the sadness and anger with our laughter. Essence sits on her bed and says, "Do you guys remember that night we all stood in the middle of my bed, hollering for hours?"

I feel jittery just thinking about it. "That mouse was strolling all over your room. Just roaming around like he lived here," I say.

"He did live here!" Nikki says.

And we laugh harder.

I finish the story, "And Dad teased us. Said we were scaredy-cats."

Nikki remembers, "Yeah, he was like, 'You three tall girls are scared of a tiny mouse?' "

"If it wasn't for your dad," Essence says, "I don't know what we would've done."

She is talking about how Dad came and put out mousetraps, how he always comes and helps—fixing things around her house like he's the handyman. She is talking about how Dad came the night Ms. Jackson had a breakdown and locked herself in the bathroom, how he called Mom and how they took Ms. Jackson to the hospital and let Essence stay with us until her mom was better.

Just as quick as the laughter came, it leaves. Essence stands up and paces the room with her arms folded. "I can't believe I have to move. I hate our landlord," she says. "I really hate him. He kept telling us he was going to redo the basement. Every year he had some plan, telling us he could make it a rec room, a study, an exercise space, but it's still just a creepy dungeon," Essence says. "And then he has the nerve to start fixing things—right in our faces—a new bathroom with a jetted tub and marbled shower." Essence fills a suitcase with the clothes that are hanging in her closet. "And he goes and tells us it ain't for us. Like we ain't good enough to live in a place like this. Can you believe that? He's going to fix it all up, and we can't stay." She inhales a gulp of air. "He knew he was going to sell the house. He knew it. And he knew we wouldn't be able to afford it!"

Essence looks out of the window. "Just when things are starting to get nice around here, too. Finally got a neighborhood I don't have to be afraid to walk through at night, and I got to leave."

Essence sits back on her bed. I don't know what to say, what to do. I am just as mad as she is, but it won't do any good to join her in complaining. Nikki and I start taking her posters off the wall. Most of them are pages Essence tore out of hair magazines, except for the one big poster of her favorite basketball player.

The last things left to pack are the picture frames on her dresser. Every photo has a friend in it. There's one of her and Malachi, and another of her, Nikki, and me when we were in the eighth grade. We are standing outside the Oregon Museum of Science and Industry at a field trip. The three of us just happy to be together.

The next frame Essence picks up holds a picture of us at the Tillamook Cheese Factory. Ms. Jackson is standing on the end, holding her waffle cone. The rest of us had all gobbled ours right before my mom took out her camera. Mom and Ms. Jackson used to take us to the coast every summer, and we couldn't go without stopping at the cheese factory. Each year, we took the tour to see the huge machines and learn how cheese is packaged, how ice cream is made. At the end of the tour, we'd stop by the gift shop. Mom always bought smoked cheddar; Ms. Jackson, the squeaky cheese curds that make noise as you chew. And at the very end, we all got ice cream cones—the best part of the day.

Essence gently puts the photo in the box. There is no bubble wrap to put the frames in, so she takes a black marker, writes FRAGILE on the box. I think maybe that note is not only about what's in the box, but the girl packing it.

The three of us sit, looking at the lonely room. I

think of all the things we did here. How when we were in elementary school we were small enough to fit under her bed and we would pretend to be on a camping trip. In middle school we whispered and giggled the night away talking about our secret crushes. We carved ESSENCE + MAYA + NIKKI = FRIENDS 4 EVER in her closet.

"I'm going to miss you," I say.

Nikki looks at me like I have just said the craziest thing. "You're acting like she's leaving the country."

"Well, the bus ride *is* forty-five minutes," Essence tells us. "You two better come see me."

I don't know why I start talking in a motherly tone, but I can't help it. I say, "You better keep your attendance up."

"She'll be fine," Nikki says. Like she's forgotten that Essence hits the snooze button for an hour before she crawls out of bed. We both know how long she takes to do her hair, her makeup, and to nurse her hungover mother before she leaves for school.

"Maya, don't worry about me. I've got to stay on top of things so I can get me some scholarships. Perfect attendance. Honor roll. That's my goal." Essence stands up, and we follow her downstairs. The stairs moan like an old woman with bad knees. Essence says, "I wonder when the landlord's going to fix the rest of the house. You two have to get in good with whoever moves in here so you can tell me how he changes the upstairs."

"Okay," Nikki says.

I don't say anything.

We go into the kitchen, and Essence opens the refrigerator. It is in its usual state. Half-empty. She takes out three cans of soda, and we go outside and sit on the porch swing. Essence and Nikki start talking about prom. They're already making plans even though prom is at least ten months away.

We've had our senior year planned out since we were in middle school.

Prom: Me and Devin, Nikki and Ronnie, Essence and Malachi.

College: the boys at Morehouse, us girls at Spelman.

That's the plan.

Essence and Nikki talk about going to the beach the weekend of prom, which I know Mom and Dad are not going to allow. I let them have their fantasy and start watching Essence's neighbor, Carla, who is moving another roommate into her house. Carla moved in two years ago. She's thirtysomething, at least I think she is. She rents rooms to college students, which means there are always people in and out. Carla is in a band and sometimes has rehearsals in the garage, and that always gets Ms. Jackson complaining. She thinks the music is too loud. "And it don't even sound good," Ms. Jackson always says. And then she goes on and on about it. "White people moving here thinking it's okay to play music all loud and let their dogs go to the bathroom all on the sidewalk. Let one of us blast our music and I bet they call the police for noise violation."

I guess the one good thing about Essence moving is, Ms. Jackson won't have to argue anymore with Carla.

I actually don't mind Carla's music. She even offered to give me guitar lessons, but I never took her up on it.

Carla waves at us. I wave back.

"Maya, are you listening to us?" Nikki says. "We're about to go see a movie with Ronnie and Malachi. You should call Devin and see if he wants to come."

"Today is Thursday," I remind them. And they know what that means. Devin is enrolled in Summer Scholars. He never misses it. We've been out of school for two weeks, and I've barely seen him. "Maybe we'll hang out with you guys tomorrow," I say.

When Ronnie and Malachi come to pick up Nikki and Essence, they all try to get me to come, but I refuse to be the looming shadow of a double date. "I'm fine," I tell them. I go across the street. Home.

I text Devin. Ask him if he wants to get together when his class is over and wait for him to get back to me.

CHAPTER 6

Devin is here.

But not for me.

He has a meeting with Dad. They check in once a month. Usually Dad takes him out to eat, but today he's putting Devin to work and they are pulling up the carpet from one of the rooms in the basement. I guess all the renovations on our block has Dad wanting to fix things up here, too. He promised he'd give Mom her own sewing room by the end of summer.

I can hear Devin and Dad talking, even though I'm not really trying to listen. Devin is telling Dad about his aunt and how he feels she doesn't understand where he's coming from. "It gets frustrating sometimes living in a house full of women."

Dad laughs. A little too hard, if you ask me. "Son, I know. I know."

Devin has grown up in a house full of women, and Dad says women don't know everything, can't teach a boy everything, shouldn't have to be everything. Devin's mom and dad died in a car accident when he was just a baby, and his aunt took him in and raised him as her own. His aunt has never been married and has four daughters who are older than us. They baby Devin sometimes, and a lot of times they can be bossy. He complains about it, but I think he also likes the attention.

I think Devin's family looks out for him because they know he really might do something big with his life. Devin is the one who makes sure we all keep our grades up, that none of us end up on the wrong side of the statistic. He talks about the future, has plans and dreams of what he wants his life to be.

Devin is a make-your-momma-proud kind of person. The good-grade-makin', football-all-star-playin' brotha who old women point to and say, "He's the next . . ." New hope stirring in them because when they look at Devin the future don't look too bad.

"He's a good catch," Mom always tells me.

And women throughout our neighborhood pull me aside, saying things like, "I'm glad he's dating you and not one of *them*." And by *them* they either mean a white girl or a hood girl. I guess Devin and I are some kind of prize to each other.

But sometimes, instead of winning a prize, I feel like I'm losing him. He always has an excuse, always a reason for not hanging out. At first I thought maybe he was cheating on me. But I trust him, and I know he's telling me the truth when he tells me he can't spend time together because he has to get up early for his Summer Scholars program. He is on a mission to be the first in his family to go to college, to be something other than a Portland guy who *could have* been something. There is no other girl. Just his dream.

How can I compete with that?

CHAPTER 7

Essence's landlord finished the rest of her house after she moved out. For two weeks, construction workers came early and stayed late. It's the Fourth of July weekend, and now the house has a FOR SALE sign in front of it. Today is the open house where people come and walk through to decide if this is where they want to live.

I don't belong here. I am the only black person in the entire house. Probably the only one who has lived in this neighborhood my whole life.

The Realtor makes the guests take their shoes off at the door. They *ooh* and *ahh* like tourists in a new city. I pretend like I am looking, like I have never been in this house before. And in a way, I haven't.

It is strange to feel like a stranger in my best friend's home.

The hallway is painted a pale tan color, and the carpet has been replaced with hardwood floors. Nothing looks regular anymore. Everything seems special—even the knobs for the shower and sink in the bathroom look like they were handpicked, especially chosen for this new house.

I step out of the bathroom and walk down the hallway to Essence's bedroom. There is a girl coming out of it. "I love it, Mom," she says. "We have to get this one."

"It is pretty great," her mom says. "Perfect for your dad getting to work. Carver Middle School isn't too far from here."

They both have brown hair. The mom's hair is cut short with curls that flip and twirl all over her head. The girl's hair is straight and hangs to the middle of her back. They both have on the same color of nail polish. Makes me wonder if they paint their nails together and gossip about the happenings of the day.

"Where are Dad and Tony? Have they been up here yet?" The girl grabs her mom's hand and they walk down the stairs.

I walk into Essence's bedroom. It looks bigger without her bed and dresser in here. I walk over to the window that faces the street and look out at my house. I remember how sometimes, when we talked on the phone, Essence would stand at her bedroom window and I'd stand at mine and we'd talk while looking at each other. Mom called us crazy.

I walk over to the closet, and when I open it, I know exactly why that girl loves this room so much. Even the closet has been renovated. It's a walk-in closet now—shelves and room to stand in and take your time to choose what it is you want to wear. Space, space, and more space so that your clothes aren't bunched up on each other, getting wrinkled.

I think about Essence, how she would love this closet.

From the hall, I can hear people roaming from room to room, plotting out how they could make this house their home. "We could use this for an office," I hear a man say about the room across the hallway.

There are many conversations swirling through the house.

This is an up-and-coming neighborhood.

Is there a Whole Foods in the area?

What are the neighborhood schools?

This is a prime location.

Is it a child-friendly neighborhood?

The crime rate has gone down.

"You like the closet, too, huh?" a male voice asks. His voice is closer than those in the hallway. I turn to see who he is talking to, and I realize he is talking to me. It's just the two of us in the room. He is standing close enough to me that I can smell his cologne, or maybe it's the leftover fragrance of his shampoo. He smells like soap, like a freshly washed load of laundry. "Sorry, didn't mean to scare you," he says. "I, uh, I came up here looking for my sister. She said I had to come see upstairs."

"Oh, don't worry about it. I was just about to leave."

"Tony?" A tall man walks into the bedroom. He is with the brown-haired girl and her mom. They crowd into the room, looking at every single detail. The light fixtures, the windowsill, the crown molding.

I take another look at the closet and notice that ESSENCE+MAYA+NIKKI=FRIENDS 4 EVER has been covered with a fresh coat of paint.

I leave.

Just as I step into the hallway I hear the mom say, "Honey, we should make an offer. Seems like it was made just for us."

CHAPTER 8

The boy who moved in across the street has Essence's room.

He hasn't put up curtains yet, so I see him all the time. Sometimes without even trying.

I can't remember his name.

He has the same brown hair and green eyes as his mom and sister. His shoulders are wide, and they hide under a too-big T-shirt.

The only thing I know about him is that he likes art. I've been watching him hang framed paintings on his bedroom walls—covering up all that fresh-paint newness. Not even appreciating that he has beautiful, clean walls that don't need to be covered.

Essence hung posters over parts of the wall that had chipped paint, small holes, cracks.

CHAPTER 9

I am sitting on the porch when I see the boy who lives across the street walking toward me. He has a look in his eyes like he knows me. "Nikki?" he asks.

I smile. "Maya."

He steps back. "Oh, I'm sorry. You look like—"

"She's my twin," I tell him.

"Oh! Oh, wow, I-I didn't know. She didn't even—"

"Yeah, we don't really mention it unless we're standing next to each other."

"You two look just alike," he says.

"We're identical."

"Right. Oh, and, uh, I'm Tony Jacobs."

"Nice to meet you," I say. "Nikki isn't here."

"Okay. I, uh, I was just looking for my sister. I thought they were together."

"Yeah, Kate, right? They just left not too long ago. Nikki is showing her the neighborhood."

I feel like I need to say something, give a reason why I didn't go, but instead I just smile at him. Nikki invited me, but I refused to go meet and greet the people who moved into Essence's home. Funny how I ended up meeting them anyway.

Just when I am trying to find something to say, Tony jumps back, like a thought just shocked his body. He squints and says, "Wait. So that was you. No wonder your sister looked at me like I was crazy when I brought it up the other day. It was you I saw at the open house."

I laugh.

"So, was your family thinking of moving across the street, or did you just want to spy on who your new neighbors would be?"

"Well, we weren't thinking about moving."

Tony laughs. "I would have done the same thing."

"So, are you from Portland?" I scoot over and make room for Tony to sit down on the step.

"Yeah. I grew up in Northwest Portland." Tony sits next to me. "We moved because my parents wanted to be closer to their jobs."

"What do they do?"

"My dad teaches at Carver Middle School. My mom writes grants for a nonprofit whose mission is to reform public schools." Tony swats at a fly. "If it were up to my mom, we would have moved over here a long time ago. She thinks it's important for my dad to live in the community where he's teaching. This year she decided to put her children where her mouth is, so I won't experience my senior year at St. Francis and my sister won't finish her last two years there. Kate and I will be going to Richmond High."

"I'd hate to have to transfer my senior year."

"Especially to Richmond," Tony says. And he says *Richmond* like it's a poisonous word.

"I go to Richmond," I tell him. "Both of my parents went there, too." I move my twists from one side to the other. "Must be nice to have the luxury of experimenting with your education," I say. I scoot away from him without meaning to.

Tony's face turns red. "Hold on. Wait. I didn't—I mean, I don't think I—"

"You didn't mean it like that?"

"Not at all."

They never do.

"I'm sorry. You must think I'm a jerk," Tony says. "Um, look, I just meant that it's going to be very different going to a public school—no matter what public school, not just because it's Richmond."

I don't say anything.

"I didn't mean to offend you," Tony says. "Can,

can we—? Okay. I'm hitting the rewind button." Tony actually sticks his hand in the air and presses down as if he's pushing a button. He makes a noise with his mouth like he's erasing what he just said.

I can't help but smile at how pitiful he looks.

"Okay, good. You're smiling. Smiling means you're not mad," he says. "Can we start over?"

CHAPTER 10

Of all the good restaurants we could go to, Nikki wants to take Kate to Popeyes—which is a surprise because lately all she wants to do is eat at the new restaurants on Jackson Avenue. But ever since Kate and Tony moved across the street, we've become their Northeast Portland tour guides, so here we are standing in line for chicken and biscuits.

Kate says to us, "You are so lucky that you grew up over here. We didn't have a Popeyes anywhere near where I lived. We used to make special trips just to have an excuse to come here."

Is she serious?

"I love soul food," Kate says.

"Popeyes is *not* soul food," I say. And I must've rolled my eyes because Nikki gives me a look that tells me to be nice and to stop looking at Kate like that. But I've had enough of Kate and her love for crispy chicken, her admiration of my braids, her excitement about all the boutiques to shop at that are just steps away from our homes.

She is a nagging fly that hovers and hovers. We've spent the last two days with her, and all she's done is ask me questions.

About my hair: "How long does it take you to get your hair like that? Can I touch it?"

About my skin: "So, this might sound like a stupid question—but do you get sunburned?"

About Richmond High: "Have you ever seen anyone get shot?"

And when we got caught in a rain shower she just couldn't understand what the big deal was when Nikki and I ran for cover. "It's just rain," she said.

I told her, "Rain is like kryptonite to a black girl's hair."

We laughed about it, but I could tell she had more questions.

We order and sit at the table closest to the door. Kate bites into her spicy chicken sandwich. "Oh. My. God. This. Is. So. Good." She takes another bite. "This just made my day."

Nikki eats a handful of fries and says, "Just wait for dessert. I want to take you to that frozen yogurt place. You can put whatever topping you want on it. So good."

Kate looks at me. "Are you coming?"

"Uh, no. I have plans with Essence." I look at Nikki. "*We* have plans with Essence."

"But you love ice cream," Nikki says to me.

"Right. Ice cream. Not frozen yogurt." I can't help but sound irritated. "And Essence will be waiting for us." This is the third time this month that Nikki has canceled or changed plans on me and Essence.

"Do you want to come, Tony?" Nikki asks.

"I'm with Maya on this one," Tony says. "If you want ice cream, you've got to get the real stuff. That watered-down version just doesn't compare."

Nikki whispers to Kate, "They're just anti–anything healthy."

Kate laughs.

"That's not true!" I fight back.

"Well, why won't you try that new vegan restaurant with me?" Nikki asks.

"I already told you why I'm not going to those restaurants." I look at her hard. Long. *Don't go there right now, Nikki. Don't.* She already knows how I feel about all these white people coming over here opening up their shops in our neighborhood. She knows how many black entrepreneurs couldn't get business loans from the bank. Dad and Mom talk about it all the time.

I look at my phone to check the time. "If we don't leave soon, we're going to be late. You know it takes forever to get to Essence's," I say.

"I can take you," Tony says.

Before I can respond, Kate says, "Can you drop us off at the fro-yo place first?"

"Kate, it's like three blocks away," Tony answers.

"More like ten," Kate says.

Tony sighs. "Yes, I can take you."

Kate takes the last bite of her sandwich. "Thanks."

We walk to the parking lot and a car pulls up beside us, real slow. I know the car because of the license plate. Roberto Sanchez. His license plate is personalized with his football number, and he has two bumper stickers of the Mexican flag on his car. He rolls his window down. "Ey, Maya, what's up?"

"Hi, Roberto."

Nikki puts her hand on her hip. "Is that all you see?"

Roberto puts his car in Park and gets out. "You get a hug," he says. He opens his arms wide. They hug, and I hear him whisper to Nikki, "So does your friend have a boyfriend?"

Nikki laughs and grabs Kate's arm, pulling her closer. "Kate, I want you to meet someone."

Tony steps forward, stands right next to Kate. Is that what it feels like to have a big brother?

Nikki introduces Tony to Roberto, and then a car starts honking because Roberto's car is blocking traffic. Roberto gets in his car but not without asking Kate for her number. She is red-faced and smiley and gushing with new crush joy.

The man honks his horn again.

"Kate, let's go," Tony says. He walks over to his car. I follow him. Nikki stays behind to play matchmaker.

When Kate gets to the car, she opens the back door and gets in. "Maya, you can get in the front. I don't want Tony to feel like a chauffeur when I get out."

I get in and Tony starts the car.

Kate talks the entire ten blocks. "So what do you know about Roberto?" she asks.

"He's hilarious. His bark is bigger than his bite, or whatever the saying is," Nikki says. "You should definitely call him."

"What grade is he in?"

"He's a senior."

Kate actually is quiet for a moment—just a moment. Then she says, "Tony, don't say anything to Dad."

Tony looks in the rearview mirror.

"I mean it, Tony."

Nikki butts in. "You're not allowed to date?"

I notice Tony's eyes again, looking at Kate in the rearview mirror.

"My dad is overprotective, too," Nikki says. And she goes into the story about when Dad found out she was dating Ronnie. Kate listens to the story, laughs when Nikki tells the part about Dad texting Ronnie a "friendly reminder" of Nikki's curfew an hour before he was supposed to drop her off. "It's so hard dating guys at Richmond because my dad pretty much mentors them all."

Tony's mind seems to be somewhere else, and I have a feeling that the look he gave Kate was about more than how funny and protective their dad can be. I know that certain looks from one sibling to another mean something.

Tony drops off Nikki and Kate.

"So where does Essence live?" Tony asks.

"All the way past St. Johns Bridge. You can drop me off at the bus stop. You don't have to take me all the way."

"It's fine. I don't mind," he says.

"Are you sure?"

"It's fine," Tony says. "Really."

"Thanks."

Tony turns the radio on. He dials through the stations until he finds one that is not playing a commercial.

We're not even halfway down the block when my phone vibrates in my pocket. I pull it out. It's a text from Essence. *Don't come. My mom is trippin' today.*

I text back. *U OK? Call me later.* And then I say to Tony, "Um, sorry, Tony, change of plans."

He stops at the red light. "So where do you want me to take you?"

"Home, I guess."

"Home? Let's go get ice cream."

CHAPTER 11

"Is there a Baskin-Robbins around here?" Tony asks.

"No. But we have some pretty good ice cream shops in the area," I tell him.

"Oh, yeah, my mom mentioned a place that's on Jackson Avenue. It has like, different flavors you might not think of for ice cream. Like Lavender Honey and Strawberry Champagne." He's talking about the new ice cream parlor that opened at the start of summer. It always has a line wrapped around the block.

I tell Tony, "The best place around here is Cathy's Cones. It's not fancy and the flavors are pretty regular, but it's good."

"Okay. Let's go there."

When we get to Cathy's Cones, we are greeted by the dry-erase board that has QUESTION OF THE DAY written at the top. Today's question is, WHAT WAS YOUR FAVORITE CARTOON GROWING UP? I grab two markers and hand one to Tony. "You have to answer the question of the day before you can order."

Tony writes SPONGEBOB SQUARE PANTS. His handwriting is neat and in all caps.

I write RUGRATS next to THE PROUD FAMILY and above THE FLINTSTONES.

Once we order our ice cream, the questions continue. Tony and I get to know each other and realize that besides our love for ice cream, we both like Thai food. Both hate black licorice but love the red kind.

"So, have you started your college search yet?" he asks.

"I've pretty much known where I've wanted to go since I was in middle school," I tell him. "Spelman."

"Where is that?"

"It's in Atlanta. It's an all-girl, historical black college," I tell him. "What about you? What colleges are you looking at?"

"First choice is Stanford. I did their summer intensive for high school students last summer, and I loved it," Tony says. "If I don't get in, I'll probably go to U of O."

"I really hope I get my first choice," I tell him.

"You have a major in mind?"

"Journalism."

We eat our ice cream and people-watch. Tony is eating faster than I am. He is almost finished with his pralines and cream, and I am just getting to my second scoop of coffee.

"So you must like to write. I mean, if you want to be a journalist."

"The writing is okay, I guess," I explain. "But I love investigating. I've always liked asking questions, finding deeper reasons and meanings for things."

"So besides writing, what else do you like to do?"

"Um—"

"You have to think about what you like to do?"

I laugh. "I don't know. I like to do a lot of things."

"First things that come to mind. No hesitating. Name three things you like to do," Tony insists.

I feel like I'm on a game show.

Tony clears his throat. "I'll go first," he says. "Three things I like to do: watch movies, hike, and make beats. I'm really into music. Your turn." He waits for my response.

"Okay. Sing—I actually love to sing and listen to music. And, uh, I like to watch movies, too," I say.

"You sing? Can I hear something?"

"No! I'm not just going to start singing."

"Why not?" Tony laughs.

"I don't just sing for people."

"Well, will I ever get to hear you sing?"

"Maybe at school. I sing for assemblies and sometimes at our games."

"So you're going to make me wait until school starts?" Tony gives me sad eyes but then smiles.

I change the subject. Way too much attention is on me right now. "So, you like movies," I say. "Drama or comedy?"

Tony scrapes the bottom of his foam cup and takes one last bite of his ice cream. "I pretty much like any kind of movie."

"Even the old black-and-white classics?"

"Especially those," Tony answers.

"Do you like Alfred Hitchcock?" I ask.

"That man was a genius! I have a DVD collection of his show, *Alfred Hitchcock Presents*," Tony says.

"For real? I love Hitchcock, too," I tell him. "I used to watch his show with my grandmother all the time."

"My dad had me watching Hitchcock when I was a kid. My mom hated it."

"Why?" I ask.

"My mom gets paranoid about everything. She thought I was too young to watch that kind of stuff. I think she was afraid it would screw me up." Tony wipes the corners of his mouth with a napkin. "Who knows? Maybe it did." He looks at me with evil eyes and a devilish smile.

I laugh. Even though I'm full, I finish the last few

spoonfuls of ice cream in my bowl. "So what about you? What do you want to be?"

"Well, if I have a choice, some kind of music engineer or studio tech guy."

"What do you mean, 'if you have a choice'?"

"Long story. My dad, he thinks, he says music is a waste of time. He, yeah, my dad, he just isn't that, he's not that supportive." Tony backs away from the table, looks at the line that's forming at the counter. "We should give up our seats. It's getting crowded."

I say okay even though the line isn't that long. Even though I want to stay and talk with him more. I look at Tony, with his nothing-special green eyes and his messy brown hair. Tony, whose mother is on a mission to save the black and brown children of the hood. Tony, who gets tongue-tied when talking about his dad. He's awkward but kind of funny. And he likes movies. Good movies.

My journalist mind is full of questions now, and I have something new to investigate: Who is Tony Jacobs?

CHAPTER 12

Summer's sun simmers in the sky. Last night I barely slept it was so hot. Toss and turn, turn and toss. That was my whole night until finally I woke Nikki up so I could have some company. We ate Popsicles one after the other until our tongues were tie-dyed rainbows. When we were too tired to stay awake but too miserable to sleep, she brought her fan into my room and we had double the air so we finally fell asleep.

Now I'm in the shower and Nikki is in front of the mirror flat ironing her hair. The smell of the smoke fills the bathroom and competes with the fragrance of my citrus body wash. "I don't know what to wear to Essence's birthday party," Nikki says. "What are you wearing?" Her voice sounds muffled because of the running water.

I push the lever and the shower water becomes a fountain gushing out into the tub. I turn the knob to the left and the water stops. "I don't know yet."

"I was thinking about wearing a dress, but that's probably too much, right? What about jeans—would that be too casual?"

I open the shower curtain halfway and reach for my towel so I can dry off. "Why don't you wear—"

"I mean, I guess a skirt would be fine, you know, instead of a dress. I don't know, Maya, I might not go."

"Nikki." I step out of the tub, wrapped in my towel.

"I'm serious." Nikki scoots over to make room for me at the mirror.

"All those clothes you have and you can't find anything to wear?" I stick about four bobby pins in my mouth and start pinning my twists up.

"Well, you know how they can be. Essence's family is—"

"No one there is going to judge you, and if they do, who cares?" I slide a pin in my hair, leaving half the twists down in the back.

"That's easy for you to say. Your hair is acceptable to them, and no one thinks your clothes are weird."

The last time we got together with Essence and her cousins, they gave Nikki a hard time because she perms her hair. And once they realized they could get under her skin, they talked about her thrift store clothes and free-spirited style. One of Essence's cousins said, "Girl, you too much for me. What you trying to be, white or something?"

Both Essence and I stood up for Nikki, but ever since then she opts out of any gatherings they're going to be at.

"You have to go, Nikki. It's her birthday. And anyway, I twist my hair because I hate the maintenance of permed hair. My hairstyle is not making a political statement."

"Well, I know that," Nikki says. "But they treat you like some kind of black princess of the Nile."

We laugh.

Nikki pulls the plug to her flat iron out of the wall. "I mean, they really just don't like me. When you talk, they say how smart you are. When I talk, they say I talk white. I'm just not black enough for them, I guess."

"Do you hear what you're saying?"

"Do you remember last time we ate breakfast at her aunt's house? The lady just about fainted when I told her I don't like grits." Nikki lines her lips and then puts on lip gloss. "And they—"

"It's her birthday," I remind her.

"Well, I can take her out for ice cream or something, just the two of us. I don't want to deal with them today." Nikki blots her lips on a square of tissue and leaves the bathroom. "I'm not going."

I look in the mirror, at my thick twists.

Black Princess of the Nile.

When Nikki said it, she made it sound like a bad thing, but actually, I kind of like that name.

CHAPTER 13

When I step inside Essence's house, the first thing Ms. Jackson does is touch my hair. "Girl, you still got that thick hair, huh?" She digs her nails to my roots and massages my scalp. "Remember when I used to do your hair? You and Nikki would just cry and cry—tender-headed and sensitive as I don't know what!" Ms. Jackson laughs. She stretches one of my twists to see how long my hair reaches. "Got hair for days, just like your mom," she says.

Essence's aunts smile at me. All of them are fanning themselves with something—loose newspaper pages, paper plates.

Ms. Jackson is fanning herself with her hand. "Essence is out back with everyone else. Too hot out there for us."

I walk through the kitchen to get to the back door.

"Help yourself to the food. There's plenty," Ms. Jackson calls out.

"Okay. Thank you." I walk outside and join Essence and the rest of her guests.

Essence is wrapped in Malachi's arms. When she sees me, she walks over to me. We hug.

"Happy birthday!"

"Thanks."

Malachi and Devin ask, "Where's Nikki?"

"She's sick," I say. I don't even look at Essence when I tell the lie.

"The six of us haven't been together all summer," Ronnie says.

Essence nudges Devin. "And whose fault is that?"

Devin gives a remorseful smile. "I know, I know, it's mostly my fault. I'm usually the one not able to make something," he says.

At least he admits it.

"But I'm here now. I wouldn't have missed your birthday, no matter what."

Essence smiles and says, "You better not have missed this. And don't let this be the last time we see you. It's summer! We need to do something together before school starts."

Devin rubs his head. "I know, I know. Summer

Scholars keeps me extra busy." Devin goes on to explain all the opportunities he's getting through Summer Scholars. Somehow the conversation gets on SATs and college applications.

Essence's cousins chime in, talking about how proud they are of Essence, how they can't wait to see her walk across the stage at graduation. "And you going to college, right?" one of them says.

"Of course she going," the other one says. "And you ain't going to be like me, Essence. No kids before you're finished with college. You hear me?"

"I hear you," Essence says.

"You hear me, Mal-a-chi? I'm talking to you, too. No having a baby before you have a degree."

Malachi looks embarrassed.

"I got big dreams for my little cousin."

Essence interrupts. "Look, it's my birthday. No college talk, no big dreams today. Just cake and ice cream." Essence walks into the house.

When she comes back outside she has plastic bowls and spoons and Ms. Jackson is behind her carrying a chocolate cake with cream cheese frosting. The whole time Ms. Jackson is walking to the card table, she's saying, "I made this myself. Made it from scratch for my baby."

The rest of the adults that were in the house come

outside. Ms. Jackson lights the big candle in the middle of the cake.

Even though Essence said there'd be no dreaming today, I swear I see her lips whisper a wish just before she blows the candle out.

CHAPTER 14

I'm sitting on my bed painting my nails and listening to music when Nikki barges in. "Can I borrow your earrings?" she asks as she puts one of my silver hoops into her left ear.

I don't even bother to answer.

"We're all going to Last Thursday. You want to come?"

Why does she even bother to ask? If I have no interest in going to shops on Jackson Avenue during regular business hours, what makes her think that I'd want to go for Last Thursday, when they have sidewalk sales down the whole street and close off the blocks to cars? "No," I answer. "I'm going with Essence to the center to help Dad make registration packets for fall enrollment."

"It's going to be fun, Maya. You can't waste your whole summer volunteering with Dad."

"I've had fun this summer. You just haven't been there." That probably came out wrong, but I keep talking. "Essence and I went to the movies yesterday, and I'm going to Seaside this weekend with her and her cousins."

"Well, you should come just for the people watching alone. It's hilarious sometimes: what people have on, their crazy hair. Last month we saw someone walking his pet pig—on an actual leash." Nikki laughs at the memory.

I don't say anything.

Nikki interprets my silence. "Why don't you like Kate?"

"I never said I didn't like her."

"Well, you're always giving her attitude—"

"Well, she's always asking me questions and making offensive comments. You know, kind of like how you feel about Essence's cousins."

"Oh, come on, Maya. So just because I didn't go with you to Essence's party, you're not going to come with me?"

"You weren't coming with me. Essence invited you. We're both her best friends. Or at least we used to be."

"Look, this isn't about Kate or Essence," Nikki

says. "You should come out to get to know our neighborhood. Some of these places have been here for—what?—four years now, and you've never set foot in them. For someone who loves her community so much, you sure don't support it."

"Nikki, those places aren't here for us. You know that, right?" I get off my bed and stand at the window. I can see Essence's house, all new and fancy with its flowerpots hanging above the banister. And I think about all the new places around the corner. "I mean, really, a Doggie Daycare? How many of our friends' parents can afford daycare for their children, let alone their pets?"

Nikki just lets out a sigh and walks away, back across the hall to her room.

I follow her. She started this conversation. She can't just walk away.

Before I say another word, she says, "Okay, Maya. I get it. Just drop it. You don't want a nice, clean neighborhood. You'd rather drive all the way downtown for a good restaurant or get on the bus to go to the mall. You don't want—"

"Are you serious right now? Did I say I didn't want those things?"

"Well, that's how you're acting."

"I want things to be fair. And something is not

fair when black men and women are turned down for business loans over and over again, but others aren't."

"Maybe they just didn't qualify, Maya. Have you ever even considered that?"

"I would believe that if it was just here, in Portland. But Grandma says the same type of thing happened in Atlanta, and Dad was just talking about his friend in New York who said it's happened in Brooklyn and Harlem. That can't be coincidence. There is something—something that has allowed this to be normal, that poor communities get remade and their people are forced to move. Have you ever seen it the other way around? Ever?"

Nikki has no answer for this, so she just ignores me and keeps getting ready.

I go into my room, close the door. My nail polish is smudged now, and I'll have to take it off and start over.

I hear her as she leaves. Hear her run down the steps, hear the door shut, hear the gate clink after she closes it. I get back up and stand at the window. Nikki walks across the street to Kate's house and rings the doorbell. When Kate comes to the door they hug like they've been friends for more than a few weeks.

I sit back on my bed and start regretting the way I spoke to Nikki. I know it seems ridiculous for me not to want to shop on Jackson Avenue. Of course I like the fact that just around the corner there are all kinds of places I would have never even thought of. Like the store where you can make your own stationery or the restaurant that has only grilled cheese sandwiches on the menu—any kind of cheese you can think of, they have it. I like the fact that I can walk home in the dark from the bus stop and not feel the need to look over my shoulder, because for some reason it just feels more safe.

But for all the things I like, I can't help but wonder why the changes we've always wanted in this community had to come from other people and not us.

I don't understand why Nikki doesn't get that, why she doesn't get me.

CHAPTER 15

I take off the nail polish and just as I am about to apply a new coat, Devin's name is flashing on my cell phone. I answer it.

"Please come with us to Last Thursday," he says.

"You're going?"

"Yeah. Summer Scholars ended today. I don't have class tomorrow. I thought you were going, so I walked over here. We're all at Ronnie's. You should come. I want to see you."

Even though I have my reasons for not wanting to go to Last Thursday, there are more reasons why I want to see Devin. I can't believe I'm saying this. "I'll meet you guys at Thirteenth and Jackson."

"Okay."

I hang up the phone and rush to find something to wear.

By the time I get to Jackson Avenue, everyone else has already made it. I'm surprised that Tony isn't here; for some reason, I just assumed he was coming. Malachi and Essence aren't here either. They went to the movies instead. So it's me and Devin, Nikki and Ronnie, Kate and Roberto.

There are people packed onto every inch of Jackson Avenue. Besides the permanent shops that are open, there are also street vendors selling all kinds of products—from homemade soaps to jewelry. I see a man sitting at a table with a cloth draped over it. He has earrings, bracelets, and necklaces laid out on the table. He is the only black vendor out here. He smiles at me, waves at me to come over. Devin and the rest of the group go into Ray's Records. I stay outside and look at the jewelry. "This jewelry is from Ghana," he says.

I look at his collection and immediately go to the silver section. There's a necklace that has a bird with its head turned backward, taking an egg off its back. I look at it, pick it up.

"Would you like to try it on?" the man asks.

I put it on.

He gives me a hand mirror so I can see how it looks. "It's beautiful on you," he says.

"Thank you." I move the mirror backward and forward, looking at the necklace and trying to imagine wearing it with different clothes. "I like it," I tell the man. "I'd like to get it." I pay for the necklace, and the man hands me a small velvet pouch for me to keep it in.

When Nikki sees it she completely overreacts. "Maya Younger actually purchased something on Jackson Avenue," she says.

"Yeah, from the only black person on the whole street," I say.

She ignores my comment and lifts the necklace. "It's really pretty," she says. "I'll have to borrow that."

"You better buy your own while we're here," I tease.

"Whatever!"

I wave to the man with jewelry from Ghana.

We walk around for about an hour and then decide to get something to eat. Devin takes my hand, and we make our way through the crowd to Nikki's favorite new burger spot. "We have to order a basket of sweet potato french fries. The best," she says.

The line at the restaurant is out the door, but we wait anyway. Just about every restaurant is at capacity, so it's going to be a wait no matter what.

A chubby white woman types Nikki's name into her iPad and hands us a few menus. As we wait outside, a man in overalls with no shirt walks up to the restaurant. He has a lopsided, dried-out jerry curl, and his feet—the biggest feet I've ever seen—are bare and callused. He's pushing a shopping cart that is overflowing with stuff, stuff, and more stuff. I've seen him around the neighborhood my whole life.

We call him Z.

Most people assume Z is homeless, but he's not. Z lives on Eleventh Street, and his front yard looks just like his cart. I used to be afraid of him, but really, Z is the person you want on your side. I've seen him break up a fight between two rival gang members and save a little girl who almost got hit by a car before a four-way stoplight was put up.

Z stands in front of the hostess. "I need to wait in line to use the bathroom? I just need to use the bathroom."

"I believe there's a port-a-potty down the block, sir," the woman says.

"But your restaurant got a bathroom, don't it?"

"Yes, sir. But our restrooms are for paying customers only, sir."

"Who said I ain't paying? I just need to use the bathroom first. I'm gonna order something."

"Sir!" A woman behind me steps forward. She is white and tall and thin like rice paper. "You're holding up the line. We need to put our names on the list." She has a little girl with her, about seven years old. "And your cart is in the way."

I can tell the woman is holding on to her daughter's hand tightly. Her knuckles are red.

"I ain't bothering nobody. I just had a question."

"She answered your question. You're holding up the line. If you have to use the restroom, go down the block like everyone else."

Other people join in the complaining.

Z exaggerates a moan. "Ahhh, kiss my ashy toes!" He flips the line off and walks away, pushing his cart and bumping into people.

I watch him make his way down the block. He passes the man with a pet pig on a leash, and on the other side there's a woman walking on stilts. An old guy is riding a unicycle down the street, swerving and zigzagging through the people like a flying bee. I see a girl with rainbow hair cut into a Mohawk, walking up to people asking if she can do magic tricks for them.

The woman behind me sighs and says to someone next to her, “I wish there was a way to keep crazy people from coming to these things.”

I have a feeling she’s talking about Z. Not about the rest of them.

CHAPTER 16

It's the last weekend of summer vacation.

Devin is coming over, and Mom is making a big deal about this. I am in the kitchen getting some snacks to take into our family room. Mom watches me go back and forth and then says, "So I want you to keep the door open, and I don't want any—"

"Mom!"

"I'm just saying. I know how it is to be young and—"

"Mom!"

"Okay, okay." She laughs and takes chocolate chip cookies out of the box and spreads them out on a small plate. I dump half a bag of chips into a bowl.

The doorbell rings, and Dad opens the door. I hear him ask Devin how Summer Scholars was, and

I know they will be talking for a while. Mom helps me carry the rest of the snacks to the room. Before she goes back to the kitchen, she whispers, "I'll tell your dad to keep it short. They can talk college stuff later." Then she turns and says, "Now remember, I don't want any—"

"Oh, my goodness, Mom. For real."

"All right, I'll leave it alone." She smiles and laughs all the way down the hall.

Twenty minutes pass before Devin comes to the family room. He sits next to me and says, "I want to show you something." He reaches in his backpack and pulls out a Polaroid. "Look what I found," he says.

I take the picture. "I can't believe you still have this." It's a photo of us when we were in the fifth grade. Our teacher took this picture for our class bulletin board. Devin and I are standing under a sign that says APRIL STUDENTS OF THE MONTH. I remember feeling so proud. I had perfect attendance, good behavior, and stars on my chart for turning in homework on time. Nikki had been student of the month in January, and I was determined to get it, too. I remember begging my mom to let me wear my hair out—not in braided ponytails—because I wanted my hair to look nice for the picture. I wish she hadn't given in. "Look at my hair." I laugh. I have two big Afro-puff ponytails. "I look a mess." I give the photo back to him.

"You looked good," Devin says. "I was bragging to every boy in that school that I got to take a picture with the prettiest girl in the class."

"You thought I was pretty back then?"

"You still are," he says. And then he kisses me and I kiss him back, and I taste our friendship in the softness of his lips, taste playing on the merry-go-round at Alberta Park, taste snow fights in the backyard and carnival rides at the waterfront, taste the first time I saw him cry—when his cousin died—taste our remember-whens and never-forgets.

I lean my head on his shoulder, turn the TV on, and hand the remote to Devin. He flips through channels. We pass a cooking show, the news, and a talk show. Then Devin turns it to the station that plays classic black-and-white movies. He turns the channel.

I tap his leg. "Go back, go back. That was the movie *Psycho*."

"*Psycho*?" Devin turns back to the channel.

It's just starting; we haven't missed much. "Let's watch this," I say.

"I hate these kind of movies," Devin says.

"This is one of Alfred Hitchcock's best films. What do you mean you hate it?"

"It's corny. It's not scary at all. Plus, it's black and white."

"What's wrong with black-and-white movies?" I ask.

"I just don't like them."

Even though that's not a reason, I drop it. I'm not going to argue about Hitchcock.

I reach out my hand for the remote. When he gives it to me, I turn the volume down. "So you don't like Hitchcock. Well, what kinds of movies do you like?" I wonder how it is that we've known each other our whole lives but don't know what types of movies the other likes.

"Action," he answers.

"What else?"

"I don't know. Why?"

"I'm just asking. Just trying to get to know you," I say.

"You already know me," Devin says.

"I don't know everything," I say. Which is true. I know things about him, but most of the time when we're together, we're in a group. I think maybe I can find out something new about him. I learned a lot about Tony playing that game of questions. There's always something new to learn about someone, right? I clear my throat. "Okay. Answer the questions I ask you. First thing that comes to mind. No thinking," I tell him. "Milkshake or ice cream sundae?"

"It doesn't matter."

"Devin, you're not playing. Come on. Just answer the question."

He sighs. "Milkshake, I guess." He takes the control and turns the television to a sports channel. I think he's going to switch stations again, but instead, he leans back on the sofa cushions and turns the volume up.

"Devin," I whine. "Let's talk. We haven't seen each other all summer. We can't just sit here and watch TV."

I'm not even sure he hears me. His eyes are hypnotized by the screen.

Mom can stop worrying. There will be nothing going on in here at all. The magic of our kiss left just as fast as it came.

I fake a yawn.

I hear the front door open. Nikki is home. She comes into the family room, sees me and Devin sitting together. "Oh, sorry. I didn't know you had company," she says. She has the biggest grin stretched across her face. She turns around to leave.

"It's okay," I tell her. "It's just Devin."

FALL

CHAPTER 17

September.

Clouds drift in the sky like ghosts. Make you think you are seeing things and people: that one looks like Grandma's rocking chair, and that one over there a smiling face. Then a shifting and disappearing and the sky becomes a forest of cotton, a wonderland for birds, a shawl for trees.

I've been trying to catch the moment when a leaf sheds its green and turns orange or red or yellow. Most times, it happens so fast that I don't notice until the ground is covered with remnants of summer.

But this time, I am watching. Every morning, I check the tree outside my house. I want to see the process of change, not just the outcome. I want to know what it looks like when tree branches wave good-bye to summer.

CHAPTER 18

It is the first day of school.

There are news reporters at Richmond and a photographer is taking pictures of us as we enter the building. "Can I get some back-to-school smiles?" he says. A group of girls sit on the steps and pose for him.

Nikki, Essence, and I walk down senior hall on our way to our lockers. There's a man standing in the hallway. "Good morning, good morning," he shouts. "Welcome back, welcome back. We're having an assembly before classes start. Everyone to the auditorium, please. Everyone to the auditorium, please."

Nikki whispers to me, "Is that our new principal?"

I nod. "I think so."

The man keeps grinning and waving us to the

auditorium. "Welcome back," he repeats. "Hello, hello."

"He's trying too hard," Essence says.

I take a look at the man. He is short and a few pounds past skinny. He waddles when he walks and his cologne saturates the entire hallway. He is the first black principal Richmond has had since I've been a student here. "Well, I give him points for wanting to meet us. Remember Ms. Stone? She acted like we had some infectious virus. How many times did we see her in the hallways?"

Essence laughs. "Uh, never. Unless she was coming or leaving."

Principal Stone quit last year right in the middle of the day. Just cursed her staff and walked out. She was the third principal Richmond had had in the four years I've been at this school. For the rest of the school year we had a temporary principal. Most adults come to this school like it's some kind of experiment. Every year some know-it-all comes here and says he knows what will get us really caring about our education.

Every year the rules change, but nothing else.

Before we enter the auditorium, our new principal comes over to us. He looks at me and Nikki and says, "I'm seeing double." He laughs as if this is an original joke, but we have heard it our entire lives.

I reach out my hand. “Hi, I’m Maya.”

“And I’m Nikki.”

Essence introduces herself, too.

“I’m Principal Green,” he tells us. “I’m looking forward to getting to know you.” Then he looks at Nikki and back at me. “I hear there are twin sisters here, and one of them is the student body president.”

Nikki points at me. “That would be her.”

“Well, nice to meet you. I’ve heard a lot of good things about you from the teachers and staff here.” Principal Green looks at me and changes his tone to a serious one, like what he has to say is really important. “I’m really looking forward to seeing how you’ll lead the school. You ready?”

I’ve been ready since freshman year. “Yes,” I tell him. “I really want student council to do something that matters this year, not just plan dances.”

“Good, very good.”

We say our good-byes, and Principal Green tries to tell Nikki and me apart. He gets it wrong.

Nikki laughs. “That’s Maya. The one with the twists.”

Principal Green looks at our hair. “Got it. You’re Nikki, you wear your hair straight. You’re Maya, you wear twists.”

“Right,” we tell him.

“I’ll get it, I promise.”

Nikki says, "You will. Once you get to know us, you'll see how different we are."

We follow the crowd to the auditorium. Essence spots Malachi, who is sitting in the middle of the fifth row. "Let's sit there."

I search the crowd, trying to find Devin and Ronnie so they can come sit with us. But instead of finding them, my eyes land on Tony. He's sitting two rows behind me, next to a girl who is stomping and chanting, "Sen-ior Pow-er! Sen-ior Pow-er!" The rest of the senior class joins in, and soon the juniors, sophomores, and freshmen are all chanting for their class.

Principal Green comes onstage and takes the microphone off the stand. He shouts, "Are the Richmond Warriors in the house?"

We all cheer and applaud.

"All right, all right. Let's settle down." He waits until the auditorium is silent. "First off, I'd like to welcome you back to school. I am honored to be your new principal. I truly believe this is going to be a great year. We are going to prove to ourselves and to this community that the Richmond Warriors value learning and are committed to excellence."

We all clap.

He continues, "That means showing up not just for games and dances but for classes and tutoring sessions."

There are not as many cheers when he says this.

"In order to do this, we have to take care of each other. If one of us fails, we all fail. We are only as strong as our weakest link," Principal Green says. "And we can do it! We are in this together, Richmond. Each one of you needs the person beside you in order for this school to be everything it can be. Now I want you to try something with me." He clears his throat and says, "We're going to do a call-and-response chant. When I say, 'Am I my brother's keeper?' you're going to shout back, 'Yes, I am!' Okay?" Principal Green is definitely more excited about this than we are. He puts the microphone close to his mouth and yells, "Am I my brother's keeper?" He points the mic to the audience.

A few of us respond. "Yes, I am."

"Am I my brother's keeper?"

"Yes, I am."

"Come on, Richmond," he says. "You can do better than that."

"Am I my brother's keeper?"

"Yes, I am!"

"That's right, that's right! Now remember, when you see one of your peers making a bad decision, encourage them to do the right thing. We all need each other."

Principal Green gets serious when he says, "Now,

seniors, I especially want you to think about this. This is your last year. What will your legacy be?"

I look around the auditorium. Some of us are asleep, some are whispering, others have headphones in their ears. Essence has her cell phone out. She quickly types a message and slips her phone back in her pocket.

Principal Green makes a few general announcements about the new lunch schedule and introduces new staff. Then he says, "Now, I want my juniors and seniors to listen closely," and he reminds us about registering for the SAT. "Before I let you go, I want you to look at the person to your left and look at the person to your right."

There's laughing and talking.

"Seriously, seriously. Take a good look. A real good look," Principal Green says. "The person sitting to your left might not walk across the stage on graduation day. The person to your right might end up in jail, or on drugs, or dead before the age of twenty-five. That's the statistic."

The auditorium is silent except for two boys sitting behind me who keep saying to each other, "He talkin' 'bout you. He talkin' 'bout you."

"It's up to you to decide that you will not be the statistic," Principal Green says. "You all have a responsibility to continue a great legacy. People want to give Richmond a bad name, and it's up to you to change that. Young people, make us proud. Make yourself proud," he says. "Let's have a good, safe, productive year. You're dismissed."

We stand and slowly move out of the auditorium. I see Tony walking out, and I wonder if St. Francis ever had an assembly like this. Wonder if he ever had to look to his left or right and think, "This person may not make it."

And I wonder why Principal Green told us what we might not be instead of telling us the possibility of what good we could become. He just lost all the points I gave him this morning.

As we walk out, Essence asks, "Do you need an SAT score to get into community college?"

We squeeze through the crowd and make our way to our lockers. "Uh, I don't know. But you need it to get into Spelman," I say.

Essence doesn't say anything.

"Spelman is still the plan, isn't it? That's always been our plan," I remind her.

Essence says, "I have to be realistic, Maya. Portland Community College is cheaper than Spelman. Way cheaper." She takes her phone out of her pocket again. She looks at the name, sucks her teeth, then sends the call to voice mail. "If I even go to college at all."

“What do you mean ‘if’?” I ask.

Essence opens her locker, hangs her bag on a hook, and closes it.

The three of us have planned out every detail of our college years. Nikki, Essence, and I will be roommates in the dorm our freshman year and go off-campus on weekends to stay with my grandma so we can do laundry at her place and get some good home cooking. We’ve talked about moving out of the dorms and getting our own apartment our sophomore year, and by junior and senior year we’ll be interning and thinking about where we’ll go to get our masters’. Essence and Malachi will most likely be engaged by then, and Nikki and I will be her maids of honor at the wedding.

That’s the plan.

That’s always been the plan.

“We’ve been talking about going to college since we were in middle school,” I say.

Essence walks away, pulling her phone out again. “Plans change.”

CHAPTER 19

So far, the first day of school has been full of ice-breaker activities and free writes about what we did over summer break. It's lunch now, and sitting here in the cafeteria, I notice there are more white and Latino students here than last year. My freshman year, Richmond was mostly black, but in the past two years our student body has changed.

Kate and Tony are sitting with Nikki, and the rest of our crew is at a table across from the Goth girls who swear they're not Goth. Essence and I walk past their table, and I smile at one of the girls—the one with the tattoo of a star on her neck.

Essence says, "I really wish she'd let me do her makeup. That black lipstick and dark eye shadow is doing nothing for her complexion. She has such a pretty face. And her hair—the things I could do with her hair!"

As we walk up to our table, I hear Nikki saying, "Things at Richmond are never going to change. That assembly was a waste of time." She sips her flavored water. She's bringing her lunch to school now because she believes the food in the cafeteria is oppressive and damaging our bodies with each bite.

"It wasn't a waste," I say. "Well, we could have done without Principal Green's fake pep talk at the end. But he kind of had a good point about being one another's keeper."

"I don't have time to worry about nobody else," Essence says. "I got enough problems of my own." She eats a handful of fries.

Nikki says, "If people don't want to change, you can't make them. I'm here to get my education." Her eyes survey the room. She sighs. "If they don't want to get theirs, that's on them."

Every day Nikki becomes a different person.

Kate wipes her lips with her napkin. "What do you think the problem is?" she asks.

Something inside me begins to crumble when everyone at the table starts listing everything that's wrong with Richmond and nothing that is right—as if a place can't be bad and good at the same time.

Kate joins in on what's wrong with Richmond

(feeling comfortable, I guess, since everyone else is complaining). And I am wondering how it can be that a girl who has spent one day in a place can all of a sudden be an expert. "St. Francis has a multimedia literacy room with iPads and laptops that we could check out. We had a garden on our rooftop that our school lunches were made from. I don't understand why Richmond can't have those things," she says. "My math teacher told me today that I couldn't take my book home because she needed it for her other classes. I—"

"We know how bad it is," I say.

Kate's shoulders shrink. "I know you do, I just, I think—"

"Do you know why St. Francis is able to have all those things? Do you have any suggestions on how to make things better here?" I ask.

Nikki kicks me under the table, soft. I kick back, hard.

"Well, no. I, well, my, the organization my mom works for is partnering with Richmond, trying to help get more, uh, get more resources for the school."

I don't say anything, because I know nothing I say will come out right. Instead, I am looking at Devin, wondering why he is not debating with her, why he is just sitting silently. He usually gets fired up in these kinds of discussions. I follow his eyes. They are fixed on a group of girls sitting across the cafeteria. I try to see which one he is looking at, but I can't tell. I feel ridiculous right now, so I look away and try to focus on the conversation.

Then Devin turns his head, and I see him watch one of the girls get up from the table and realize that one of the new girls has caught his attention. Her name is Cynthia. She is a brown girl, but not black. She is thick in the hips with a thin waist.

Devin is so obvious.

I look away before he realizes I am watching him. I don't know where to put my eyes, so I just look right in front of me, where Tony is sitting. Our eyes lock into each other's, and I realize that while I was watching Devin, Tony was watching me.

CHAPTER 20

Cynthia.

She won't tell us where she's from. It is the last period of the day and for the sixth time today, I am playing a getting-to-know-you game. When Cynthia is introduced as a new student and is asked where she is from, she just smiles and says, "I'm from many places."

And then the guessing game starts: Is she Mexican? Indian? Hawaiian? She is a shade of brown I have never seen before. Cynthia, whose hair is the kind of curly that isn't kinky or nappy, who's thicker than skinny but not at all fat. Cynthia, who loves the attention she is getting from her guess-my-identity game. I have seen girls like her before. Back when Nikki and I modeled. Back when we were called beautiful.

We modeled when we were seven, eight, nine, ten, eleven, and twelve. Nothing major, mostly in catalogs for Fred Meyer and other local companies.

But at thirteen we found out we were just ordinary black girls. "You are not commercial enough," the agency said. Nothing exotic added to our blackness to give us unique tones, curly hair. Nothing added to our blackness to make a just-right complexion.

I haven't modeled since. Haven't felt like a nothing black girl since. But now, with Cynthia whose black is beautiful and new and different, I am thirteen again and jealous of a girl I don't even know.

CHAPTER 21

We have been in school for a month, and student council is having its first official meeting. Student council officers were voted on last school year. The official positions are:

Me	President
Charles Hampton	Vice President
Tasha Walker	Secretary
Joey Matthews	Historian
Rachel Martin	Treasurer

So when Vince and Bags walk into the student council meeting, Charles turns to me and says, "Are they serious?" He shakes his head in disapproval—and maybe disgust.

Principal Green begins our meeting, saying, "I've opened it up to other students to join our student council meetings. Even though they don't have official titles, they will help plan events this year and support our officers. I thought it would be nice to add some diversity to the group." Principal Green writes the agenda on chart paper and says, "We'll get started shortly."

I look around the room. Vince, Bags, Cynthia, and Tony have joined us. I whisper under my breath to Charles, "This is going to be interesting."

Ever since freshman year, Vince and Bags have been known as the king and prince of practical jokes. Last year, Vince put Vaseline on all the doorknobs of senior hall. Bags's real name is Noah, but we call him Bags because he always has a dime bag on him.

"Is Principal Green really going to let them be on student council?" Charles whispers in my ear. "I knew having him be our staff adviser was a bad idea." Charles is known around the school as Preacher Man. He is always dressed in khaki pants and a tie. We all joke that he is an old man trapped in a teen's body. I have no doubt he will end up at Harvard and be CEO of something one day. "We cannot let these white boys come in here with their fraternity shenanigans," Charles says.

"They'll be fine," I say.

"Famous last words."

Principal Green takes a sip of water from his plastic water bottle. "Let's begin. It's no secret that Richmond is changing. I mean, why even in this very room we can see that we have students of many ethnic backgrounds at our school. I'd like us to think of something we can do to promote diversity and celebrate all the cultures we have in our student body. Any ideas?"

No one speaks.

Not because we don't want to celebrate diversity; I just think we need time to come up with good ideas. Charles and Cynthia raise their hand at the same time. Principal Green calls on Cynthia.

She leans forward and says, "Well, Thanksgiving is next month. Maybe we could have a multicultural potluck."

Joey agrees with her. "Yeah. We could call it Tastes of the World."

Cynthia keeps adding to her idea. "And we can have food from Javier's Mexican Grill and Chinese food from Golden Wok." She barely takes a breath. "And we could get food from that new Thai place and, well, I guess we need soul food, too. Maybe Popeyes?"

Popeyes is not soul food.

Charles scoots back from the table like he wants to be as far away from Cynthia's idea as possible. "I'd like to see our budget go toward something more meaningful," he says.

I'm glad someone else said it before me. Principal Green asks me what I think. "Well," I say. "I agree with Charles."

Cynthia rolls her eyes at me. It's subtle, but I see the way she is looking at me, like she takes it personally that I don't agree with her.

"I mean, well, what does a buffet have to do with diversity?" I ask. "Most students will just come to eat. They're not going to learn anything."

Cynthia rolls her eyes at me again. This time she's less subtle. "Well, we can have an index card at each dish that gives facts about the countries represented in the buffet."

I blurt out, "You think someone's heritage can fit on an index card?" Now I'm rolling my eyes. I don't mean to be rude, and I really, really didn't mean to say it with an attitude, but is she serious? I look around the room hoping to make eye contact with someone else who might agree with me and Charles.

Tony speaks up. "But, well, isn't the school, uh, short on funds? I mean, we don't have a big budget so maybe Charles and Maya are right. We should spend our budget on something more meaningful."

Principal Green rubs his chin. "I actually think Cynthia and Joey are onto something."

"But I thought the point was to learn about other cultures, to encourage community?" I say.

Charles joins the conversation. "Yeah, what is watered-down, Americanized Mexican or Chinese food going to teach us about Mexico or China?" Charles clears his throat and in his presidential voice says, "With all due respect, Principal Green, I believe it would be best to take a vote."

"I appreciate that, Charles, I do, I do. But I think the multicultural lunch is a great idea."

"But Principal Green," I say, "we haven't heard from everyone." I look at Rachel and Tasha.

Cynthia speaks. "Come on, guys. You know people like food. I mean, it will be a great first event. We'll get a good turnout."

Principal Green adds, "And we want our first event to be inclusive. We want it to be something everyone feels welcome at and a part of."

So much for Principal Green being the neutral staff adviser.

He looks at me, then at Charles. "So why don't the two of you do some research about the different cultures that will be represented, and perhaps you can do a one-page write-up on each of them instead of the index cards. That way, it's more informative. Much more informative," Principal Green says.

"So we're really doing this?" I ask. And now *I* have a homework assignment?

Principal Green asks for volunteers to take on different responsibilities for the event. "Tony, what would you like to do?"

"I, uh, I can help Charles and Maya," he says. He looks at me. "The three of us can work together." Tony smiles.

I smile back at him and get a nervous feeling. It feels like my heart has the hiccups. This is the feeling that usually comes when I make a speech or right before I sing. And here it is, now, as I sit across the table from Tony. I look away from him, but the feeling stays.

CHAPTER 22

I'm not sure if it's a blessing or a curse that so many of us from student council are in Mrs. Armstrong's journalism class. Vince, Tasha, Charles, and Tony are all here. The best part of this class is that Essence has it, too. We're sitting next to each other, flipping through the thick packet of articles Mrs. Armstrong just passed out. "These articles need to be read by the end of the week," Mrs. Armstrong says.

The class moans.

"I keep telling you all that this is not going to be your easy-A newspaper class."

I notice a boy shift in his chair and wonder if he will transfer classes and take another elective.

"This journalism class is about investigating your world. Asking questions and doing something with the information you discover." Mrs. Armstrong has her stern voice on, but since I know her from last year, I know that, really, Mrs. Armstrong is one of the most caring teachers in this school. She's also one of the only black teachers. At the back of her classroom there's a secondhand sofa, a worn armchair, and a coffee table. If the coffee table were a person, it would walk with a limp.

We call it The Lounge.

It's a section for silent reading and writing. Sometimes Nikki, Essence, and I come to The Lounge to eat lunch and catch Mrs. Armstrong up on what's going on in our lives.

"I want you all to be investigators," she says. "Not just in class, but outside of class. And I expect you to read." She walks to the front of the classroom, checks her watch. "Are there any questions?"

Vince raises his hand. "I have a question, Miss Armstrong."

"Yes?"

"Are your arms really strong?"

"Actually, yes, Vince, they are. Remember, I'm also the volleyball coach for the girls' team. And it's Mrs., not Miss," she says.

Vince smiles at her and says, "My apologies and *sincere* regret."

Mrs. Armstrong just ignores him. Male students

are always flirting with her. She is the best-dressed teacher I've ever had. And her skin is flawless—like the women in those commercials that advertise age-defying face wash.

Mrs. Armstrong holds up a copy of *Portland's Voice*. "Any of you read the paper this morning?" she asks.

I feel bad that I haven't. Our ongoing assignment for the year is to read newspapers and magazines as much as we can. This morning, it didn't even cross my mind.

Mrs. Armstrong passes the paper around the class. The headline says, "Are Richmond Warriors Fighting Hard Enough?" There's a huge picture of a group of Richmond students sitting outside on the stoop in front of our school. The girls in the photo are laughing and talking. The picture implies that they are skipping class or just hanging out. But I remember that picture being taken on the first day of school when the press was here for the welcome-back assembly. To the side of the article, there's a chart that shows how attendance and test scores have dropped at Richmond over the years.

Mrs. Armstrong, throws the paper on her desk. "This is the third article on Richmond this school year, and it's only October. I think we should fight back. Any ideas?"

"We should give them something to write about," I say.

"They have plenty to write about. That's the problem," Charles says. His striped button-up shirt is tucked into his khaki pants and as always, he has his campaign voice on. "Low test scores, teen pregnancy, drugs, alcohol . . . oh, trust me, they have enough to write about."

Mrs. Armstrong interjects. "So you believe the hype like everyone else? Richmond is really that bad?"

Tasha raises her hand. "It's not the worst, but it ain't—I mean, it isn't the best either," she says.

I raise my hand. "But that's the problem. There are good and bad things that happen at Richmond. Just like at every other school. They never write about the good stuff. They don't want to tell that part of the story."

Charles nods in agreement. "I can see Maya's point. And I think it's wrong how everybody is blaming us for a problem that's been going on for years. Maybe if they gave us the same stuff that those other schools get, we wouldn't be doing so bad."

Mrs. Armstrong sits on her stool. "Stuff?"

Tasha jumps back in the conversation. "You know, like, other schools get new books and their teachers have supplies and stuff. What kind of mess is that?" Tasha pops her gum.

Mrs. Armstrong mouths, "Spit out your gum."

Tasha gets up and spits her gum into the garbage can.

"Anyone else want to add something?" Mrs. Armstrong asks.

I look over at Essence. She is looking at her cell phone and isn't paying attention at all to what's going on. Mrs. Armstrong clears her throat and walks over to her desk. "You know the rules, ladies and gents. No hats, no cell phones, no iPods, no nothing that can distract you or someone else from his or her education."

Essence puts her phone away.

"Anyone else?" she asks.

Essence raises her hand.

"Yes, Essence, what would you like to add?"

"Um, nothing. I have to go to the bathroom. Can I have a hall pass?"

"Can it wait?"

Essence shakes her head no. She gives Mrs. Armstrong a look, the one that says this isn't about going to the bathroom.

Mrs. Armstrong gives Essence the hall pass, and when Essence doesn't come back after fifteen minutes,

Mrs. Armstrong comes to my desk and whispers, "Go check on her."

I leave class and walk down senior hall. I go to the cleanest bathroom in the school—it's the only one that gets stocked with toilet tissue and there are always paper towels. When I step into the bathroom Essence's voice is echoing off the wall. She is yelling into her phone. When she sees me, she puts it on speaker so I can hear. The voice yelling back at her is her mother.

CHAPTER 23

"Mom, I'm at school. I can't talk about this right now!" Essence yells.

"I want to know where my money is."

"I'm hanging up now—"

"Essence, I know you took my money."

"What money?"

"You know what I'm talking about."

"Mom, I have no idea what you're talking about. I didn't know you had any money. If I did, I would have asked for it so I can get me a bus pass for the month."

"Look here, I want a hundred dollars put back in my drawer by the end of the night." Ms. Jackson sounds drunk.

I tap Essence on her shoulder and mouth silently,

"Just hang up." I know there's no reasoning with Essence's mom when she gets like this. "Hang up," I mouth again.

But Essence keeps talking. "Mom—I didn't take your money."

"As a matter of fact, I want you home right now."

"What?"

"You heard me. I want you to come home right now."

"Mom, you're drunk."

"Who you think you is, tellin' me what I am? Come home now. You hear me?"

"Mom, I'm at school."

"I don't care where you are. Home is more important than school. You said you didn't take my money, then come home and help me find it," Ms. Jackson yells.

"Mom—"

"If you don't come home right now, don't come home at all. I'ma have all your stuff outside on the sidewalk in thirty minutes if you ain't in this house."

The bell rings. Essence takes the phone off speaker before girls storm into the bathroom to look in the mirrors, spray perfume, and gossip. "All right, Mom. Okay." She hangs up.

Essence walks out of the bathroom. I follow her. "You don't have to come," she says.

"I know." I walk with her outside, down the steps, down the block, silently praying that no one sees me—Maya Younger, the student body president—skipping school. But I'm not going to let Essence go alone.

"I don't have enough bus fare for you," Essence says.

"I have enough for both of us," I tell her. I go into my bag and get money out. We ride the bus the entire forty-five minutes in silence.

When we get off the bus, on the way to her house, a group of men call out to us, flirting and trying to get us to cross the street and come talk to them. I ignore them. Essence flips them off.

When we turn the corner, I see Ms. Jackson standing on the porch in a bra and jeans throwing Essence's clothes out onto the lawn. "So you decided to come, huh?"

"Mom, go in the house. Get in the house." Essence runs up the steps and tries to push her mother inside. I start picking up the clothes. "Mom, you don't have on a shirt. Go in the house," Essence says.

"Why you always tellin' me what to do?" Ms. Jackson goes back into the house. We follow her. The house has been ransacked. The cushions from the sofa are turned upside down; books and loose paper, receipts, and mail cover the carpet. Empty alcohol bottles litter the floor. “Help me find my money!” Ms. Jackson is screaming.

“Mom. Calm down. Just calm down.” Essence goes in her mother’s room and brings out a Richmond High T-shirt. Here, put this on.”

Ms. Jackson can’t get her arm through the sleeve. I try to help her. “I don’t need your help! Your momma send you here? Huh? Your daddy told you to come check on me?” Ms. Jackson grabs a half-empty bottle from the coffee table and finishes drinking it. “Answer me, girl. They send you over here?”

“No, Ms. Darlene. They didn’t.”

Sometimes it’s hard for me to believe that Ms. Jackson and my mom were best friends when they were younger. Mom’s got all kinds of pictures of them when they were my age. I wonder why they turned out so differently. I wonder how Nikki, Essence, and I will end up.

Essence grabs the bottle from her mom.

Ms. Jackson is standing with the shirt dangling around her neck.

“Put the shirt on,” Essence yells.

“Stop tellin’ me what to do. Who you think you is, huh?” Ms. Jackson slides her arms through the sleeves.

“I wouldn’t have to tell you what to do if you

would act like my mother!" Essence starts to walk away.

Ms. Jackson yanks her back by pulling her hair. "Who you think you walkin' away from?" She is holding on tight to Essence's hair. I can't tell if it hurts or if Essence is embarrassed, but there are tears forming in the corner of her eyes.

Just as I walk over to try to pry Essence out of her mom's grip, Ms. Jackson's friend, Melvin, walks in the house. He helped them move. I think he's more than a friend, but I've never asked. Essence will tell me about him when she's ready.

Melvin is carrying four bags of groceries. He steps over the mess on the floor. "Darlene? What in the world is going on in here?"

Ms. Jackson looks at Melvin and slowly lets Essence go. "Hi, baby. Sorry 'bout the mess," she says.

Melvin hands the groceries to Essence. "Here, take these in the kitchen. Thought I'd get us some food in this house before we all starve to death," he says. "Darlene, I'll pay you back this weekend. I'll be fixing cars down at the shop so we should get some money soon."

"Okay, baby, that's fine," Ms. Jackson says. She looks at Essence. "Did you hear the man? Put the food away."

We go into the kitchen.

"And when you're finished, clean up that mess in the living room," Ms. Jackson yells. She goes into her bedroom with Melvin and closes the door.

Essence puts the groceries away. I help.

The faucet drips, the grocery bags crinkle, the cabinet doors creak open and close, creak open and close.

Essence's life is a blues song. Her mother, a scratched record stuck on the same note. I don't know what to say. I wish I could fix Ms. Jackson. Wish I knew what it would take to get her to see that her daughter is worth staying sober for. I'm so glad we graduate in June. Once June comes Essence can leave. We'll go far from here, and she never has to come back if she doesn't want to.

Essence has to go to Spelman. She can't settle for PCC. Nothing's wrong with a community college, but she has to get out of Portland. June can't get here quick enough. But I've got to figure out how to help her right now. "You want to stay at my house tonight?" I ask.

Essence shakes her head. She folds one of the brown bags. "I'd have to come home sooner or later. Can't keep running to your place," she says. "We're not little girls anymore."

CHAPTER 24

It's Friday night, and the homecoming football game just ended. Richmond won, and everyone is celebrating. The game was sold out. Students from both schools, along with alumni, teachers, parents, and community members crowded into the bleachers, bundled in scarves, hats, and gloves.

Now that the game is over, we are all standing in line to get into the dance. Ronnie and Nikki are next to each other showing way too much public affection, if you ask me.

Tony and Kate walk up to us. We let them cut the line. "Why are there so many cops out tonight?" Kate asks. "Did something happen?"

"No, they always ride around during our events," Nikki explains.

Kate blows into her hands to warm them.

Another police car creeps by.

I stand closer to Devin, take his hand.

Nikki takes a few steps forward. "Finally, the line is moving," she says.

We give our tickets to the parent volunteer at the door and step inside the dance. We mingle and talk with friends for a little while before we make our way to the dance floor. Devin pulls me close to him, and our bodies fall into a groove. We dance for two songs and then sit at a table.

"Did your dad tell you about the guy who wants to have lunch with me so we can talk about my college plans?"

I shake my head.

"He might be interested in helping me financially. He heard me speak at the fund-raising gala for the center."

"That's amazing, Devin. Have you told your aunt yet?"

Devin scoots in closer to me to make sure I can hear him over the loud music. "Waiting till I know for sure. Don't want to get her hopes up," Devin says. "You apply for any scholarships yet?"

I nod.

Devin asks me which ones I applied for and I recite the list to him, just like I do to our college counselor and every other adult who has been asking. I wiggle my toes in my too-tight shoes. Funny how I thought my feet would be hurting by this point of the night. I look onto the dance floor at the waving arms and swaying hips and see Tony dancing with a girl. He moves in sync with the rhythm of the music and when the song changes from fast to slow, he pulls her close and they wrap themselves in each other's embrace. I look away, focus on Devin.

We must not look like a couple. Maybe we just look like two friends hanging out, because Cynthia comes up to Devin—as if I'm invisible—and says, "Want to dance?" And she pulls Devin up by his arms, not even giving him a chance to answer.

"No, I'm good, I'm good," Devin says. And he backs away from her and sits down.

"Next time," Cynthia says. She smiles and walks away.

Before I can even open my mouth to go off about how much I can't stand her, Devin takes my hand and we sit and talk. At first we are laughing at how silly Ronnie looks on the dance floor doing Michael Jackson moves in the center of a circle. And then a slow song comes on. Devin leans into me, and I think he is going to ask me if I want to go back to the dance floor. But instead he asks, "So have you turned your application in to Spelman yet?"

Really? We're at a dance and you want to talk about college applications? He starts telling me about his admissions essay for Morehouse. "I'm almost finished," he says. "I made the changes your dad suggested. I just need an ending."

I had thought maybe Devin turned Cynthia down because he wanted to prove his feelings for me, show her he was mine. Thought he wanted to take me back on the dance floor, hold me in his arms all night. But instead he just wants to sit and talk. We never make it back to the dance floor. By the time Devin stops talking, it's time to go.

CHAPTER 25

I guess I was in denial, or maybe I thought I could get Principal Green to reconsider this dumb idea of a multicultural lunch. But it's really happening. There are signs about it all over Richmond.

I've been ranting about it all day to Nikki and Essence. Neither of them seems that interested in what I'm saying. And that's making me even more frustrated.

This is how it was when we were kids:

If Nikki didn't like someone at school, neither did I, neither did Essence.

If Essence was sad about something, so was Nikki, so was I.

If I was excited about something, so was Essence, so was Nikki.

So when I ask them to help me plan a boycott of the Tastes of the World buffet, I'm really not asking, I'm expecting. But neither of them cares.

Nikki says, "A boycott, Maya? Why do you always have to make a big deal out of everything?"

Essence says, "I have more important things to worry about than who's eating what, from where," she tells me. "I might not even be at school that day. Got someone's hair to do."

Essence has been skipping school to do people's hair so she can make money to pay for college application fees and other senior costs that keep adding and adding up. I can't even get on her about skipping school; at least this means she's still considering college.

Essence tells us, "I'm braiding this lady's hair and she's paying me $80. I can't pass that up."

And then Nikki says, "But tell the truth: If you weren't doing hair, would you boycott?"

Essence answers with a laugh.

CHAPTER 26

Dad hasn't been home in time for dinner all week. He called an hour ago saying he'd be here in fifteen minutes. Mom takes three plates out of the cabinet. "Let's just eat. He can warm his up," Mom says. The cabinet door slams shut. "Nikki, grab some silverware, please." Mom walks into the dining room.

Nikki gets forks and knives out of the drawer and mumbles to me, "She's going to be so lonely when we leave. Dad's never here."

I haven't thought about how Mom will feel when we leave. I mean, it's always been this way. Dad has always been off doing something for the community. When Nikki and I were ten years old, Mom enrolled us in a summer dance camp. Dad missed our recital, and Nikki cried the whole way home.

Back then, Mom said we had to share Dad. "He's the only father some of your friends have," she told us. "They need him."

She said this as if Nikki and I didn't need him, too.

"Your father is an activist," she said. She told us about the great things Dad was doing to make a change in the lives of young men and to bring about change in our community.

From that day on, I think Nikki has hated the word *activist*, and I don't think she ever forgave Dad. Mom seems to be over being the wife of a community hero. I think she'd much rather just have her husband home for dinner.

I walk into the dining room and sit at the table.

Mom takes a bite of her meatloaf. She swallows and asks, "How was school today?"

Nikki makes sure she is first to answer. "Well, Maya's trying to start a revolution." She laughs and wipes the corners of her mouth with her napkin.

Mom looks at me, expecting an answer. When I don't say anything, she says, "Well, somebody tell me what's going on."

Nikki tells her version of why I'm organizing a boycott. She gets it all wrong. "You know how Maya is, Mom. She has to make a big deal out of everything."

Mom looks at me. "Maya, are you sure you want to bring this kind of attention on yourself?"

"Dad thinks I'm doing the right thing," I tell them. I wish he were here. He'd be on my side.

Mom shakes her head. "Lord, Thomas has turned my child into a rebel."

"You used to be," I say.

Nikki looks at Mom, then at me.

"Well, she did!" I say. "Remember the letters we wrote to the city about Jackson Park?"

"That was different, Maya," Mom says.

"I don't even know what you're talking about," Nikki tells us.

Nikki gets amnesia when it's convenient.

"You don't remember the summer before fifth grade when Mom noticed that whenever we wanted to go to the park, we would ask her to drive us across town?"

Nikki doesn't say anything so I tell the whole story, even though I know she knows what I'm talking about. How could she forget something like that?

We'd pass a dozen parks driving across town. One day, Mom said she was not driving all the way "over there." That the three of us could walk to the park that was close to our house.

"But Jackson Park has no twisting slide," Nikki said.

"And the grass is so high it scratches my legs," I told Mom. "The other park has a pond and we can feed the ducks."

Mom was angry that we wanted to go to the other side of town for something as simple as playtime. So instead of going to the park that day, we wrote letters to the people in charge of parks. I didn't know there was a person deciding who gets what. But Mom knew, and she took pictures at both parks during the day and at night.

We put those photos in the envelope with our three letters and sent them off. I remember letting go of my envelope into the metal mailbox and how powerful I felt releasing my words into the world.

I remind Nikki of all this. "Do you remember now?"

"A little," she says. She drinks water from her glass and says, "What I remember most is that Mom asked every mother who had a child old enough to play at the park to write a letter and only, like, what—one or two people did, right, Mom?"

Mom nods.

Nikki continues. "Just like only a few parents show up for the meetings at Richmond, or the community forums at the center." Nikki rakes through her mashed potatoes with her fork. "I don't understand why Dad insists on standing up for people who never show up or speak up or do anything for themselves." Nikki and Mom share a look, and I know that I am not going to get them to see my side—or Dad's side. Nikki gets up from the table but continues to talk. "And Maya, I get it. I mean, I know that the buffet is a pathetic attempt at celebrating culture, but I also know that no one at Richmond really cares. You know what they care about—free food. I just don't want you to be disappointed. No one's going to boycott with you."

I can hear Nikki moving around in the kitchen—rinsing her dishes and opening the dishwasher. I look at Mom, hoping she'll have the last word, say something a mom is supposed to say, be the activist she was. But she doesn't say anything. We just sit and eat the rest of our food without speaking to each other.

After we go into the kitchen to clean our plates, Nikki starts rummaging in the freezer, looking to see if any more ice cream sandwiches are left; Mom is rearranging the plates in the dishwasher to make more space; I am playing with the magnetic words on the fridge.

Dad comes home. He walks into the kitchen, washes his hands, and immediately goes to the plate on the counter that's covered in foil. "Thanks for setting something aside for me. Sorry I missed dinner."

Mom mumbles, “Uh-huh.”

Dad kisses Mom on her cheek and warms his food. The microwave beeps, and Dad takes his dinner out. He sits at the kitchen island, takes a bite of his mashed potatoes, and says, “So how was school today?”

CHAPTER 27

Charles and I tried to get students to boycott the buffet, but Nikki was right, free food is hard to turn down. So far, it's just the two of us standing in the hallway watching everyone walk toward the cafeteria. I'm sure we won't even be missed.

The hallway clears out. I see Tony sitting at his locker eating from a bag of chips. Charles and I walk over to him.

Tony moves his books so I can sit beside him and smiles. "Not much of a boycott, but at least we're standing by what we believe," he says.

We sit next to Tony. He passes his bag of chips like Holy Communion. We eat from the bag. Senior Hall has never been this quiet. Usually there's a crowd huddled around Malachi listening to him free style, and there are cliques sitting together in front of their lockers eating and swapping gossip. But today, it seems as if every single person is in the cafeteria. A whiff from the buffet teases my nose. My stomach growls. I take a handful of chips.

The only other person in the hallway is the Goth girl with the tattoo. I have never seen her alone, away from her crew. She almost walks past us, but then she stops and stands right in front of me. "Is this the boycott?"

"Yes," I answer.

She sits down in front of me, crossing her legs. "I'm Star," she says.

I smile at her. "I'm—"

"I know who you are," Star says. She looks at Charles and Tony, like she knows them, too. "So what's the plan?" she asks.

"Plan?" Charles asks. His eyes and eyebrows bunch up and tangle in confusion.

Star grabs the bag of chips from Charles and takes a fistful. "Aren't we supposed to be protesting?"

She's got a point. "Guess we were so focused on getting people not to go that we didn't think about what we could do—or eat—instead," I admit.

Charles and Tony nod.

"So there's nothing planned? No rally, no walk-out?" Star doesn't wait for any of us to answer. She reaches into her pocket and pulls out a wrinkled piece of paper. "I thought there'd be speeches or something, so I came prepared," she says.

Charles leans back against the lockers, gets comfortable. "There can be speeches. You can read what you wrote to us."

At first Star just sits there, but once she realizes that we're really waiting to hear what she has to say, she unfolds the piece of paper and begins to read. "It's time for a change at Richmond." Star clears her throat. Her hands are shaking just a little bit, but her voice is so strong, so passionate, that we have to take her seriously. "I've gone to this high school for four years," she tells us. "My mom went here, and so did all my aunts and uncles."

Charles leans forward. Tony closes the bag of chips, quietly though, so the crinkling bag doesn't make too much noise.

Star never looks up from her speech. "My older sister went here, too, and I couldn't wait to be a Richmond Warrior. But our school isn't what it used to be. And I know Mr. Kiss-Up Green is trying to change our image, but he's just a puppet of the system. If things are going to change at Richmond, we've got to initiate that change."

Star's hands stop trembling, "I am tired of looking at chipped paint on the walls. And why are parts of our hallways missing tiles? I want to have the same options for electives that other schools have, and we need a computer lab that actually works, that we can print from because there's enough paper for everyone." Star finishes her list by saying, "And it isn't fair that I am defined by a test score. Why do the people outside of our school misunderstand us? Why does everyone keep talking about change but everything stays the same?"

For the first time, Star looks up at us. She folds the paper and slides it in the back pocket of her black jeans. "Is anyone as angry as I am?" Star asks. "What are we going to do about it?"

None of us has an answer just yet. The four of us sit on the gum-stained linoleum floor under the bright fluorescent lights and share communion until a revelation comes.

WINTER

CHAPTER 28

December.

Snow falls from the sky like confetti. At first it barely dusts the ground, making everyone go back and forth to the windows to see if it will stick. We watch the sky, wondering whether this will be the winter when we finally have enough snow to make a snowman, to flap our wings on the ground and be angels. Or will we have to drive to Mount Hood for the real winter wonderland?

At the beginning of the month, we pray to be snowed in. How many pleas for school closings does heaven hear? By the middle of the month, we realize God doesn't answer selfish prayers, because no snow has come. But we learn he has a sense of humor because it falls the day school lets out for winter vacation.

We might be snowed in for the whole break, thawed out just in time for the new year, and dry by the time classes start again.

CHAPTER 29

It's the first night of winter break. Essence is spending the night, and she isn't wasting any time getting to the gossip. "So what's up with you and Devin?"

"Nothing."

"Nothing?" Nikki calls out from across the hall. "What do you mean nothing?" She walks over to my room, still changing into her nightclothes. "You two have spent time together every night this week," she says. Then she looks at Essence and tells her, "They tell my parents they're working on *homework*—can you believe Mom and Dad fall for that?"

"I wish it was a cover-up," I say. "I mean, I'm all about getting into college, but Devin is too—"

"You're not complaining, are you?" Nikki yells. "I really hope you are not about to say Devin is not a good boyfriend because he actually has some goals for himself."

Essence interjects before I can even respond. She is styling her hair in different ways and experimenting with what her hair would look like shorter. She holds it up and looks in the mirror at different angles, then lets her braids fall down her back. "I feel you, Maya. Devin can be a little stiff at times," she says.

Nikki sits on my bed. "But isn't that better than him being someone who has no idea what he wants for his life?" Nikki asks. "That's what makes you two such a good couple. You're both so driven."

"Yeah, but—" I try to explain myself, but Essence interrupts me. She talks about how perfect Devin and I are for each other, how I'd be crazy to let him go—which I never said I was doing. I try to speak again. "What I mean is—I mean, we don't have that much in common."

Nikki and Essence tag-team me on the similarities between Devin and me.

Nikki goes first. "You both grew up in the same neighborhood."

"You're both smart."

"You're both going to historical black colleges."

"You're both black," Essence says. "I mean, do we need to say more?"

Just when I attempt to respond, Essence cuts me

off again. "Oh, *shh*, *shh*, listen." Essence turns the volume of the television up. Her favorite basketball player is being interviewed. "I love him. I swear if Malachi and I don't get married, I'm marrying him!"

She sits on the edge of my bed and turns the TV up a little more. We watch the interview, and after they talk about the basketball star's rough childhood and rise to fame, they show wedding pictures.

"What!" Essence stands with her hands on her hips. "He married a white woman?" She sits back down, shaking her head in disbelief. "That could be us one day," Essence says.

"What do you mean?" I ask.

"Ronnie, Malachi, and Devin—three young black men who are definitely going to be successful one day. What if they end up with some white girl on their arm?"

Nikki sighs. "They're not going anywhere. Yes, there are plenty of girls who want them, but that doesn't mean they want those girls. You know how it is—black boys who have something going for themselves are a rare commodity around here. But they know what they have with us. Trust me."

We watch more of the show, and when the commercial comes on, Nikki says, "We're sitting here thinking about the possibility of some other girls coming for our men—but it could be the other way around, you know. I mean, Maya has been doing *homework* with Tony, too. Maybe Devin has some competition."

Essence turns around. "And why didn't I know about this?"

"There's nothing to know," I say. "We're working on a special project for student council. Charles and Star are with us every time we get together," I explain. The four of us decided to meet over winter break so we could come up with an event to do at Richmond that Principal Green won't veto.

Nikki says, "So tell us, Maya—if you and Devin weren't together, would you ever date Tony?"

Essence turns the TV off. "Good question."

"Why would you ask me that?" I say.

"Just a question. Would you?" Nikki asks.

We used to play this game in middle school, asking who we had a crush on and who we would date. I almost always said no to Nikki's and Essence's options. They called me picky.

"Answer the question," Essence says.

"Yeah, why are you hesitating? It was just a hypothetical question, but since you're taking so long to answer, I'm wondering if Devin really does have some competition." Nikki laughs. She takes one of my pillows and holds it in her lap so she can lean into it. "We're just messing with you. We know you love Devin."

"Besides," Essence says, "if Maya isn't with Devin, she sure isn't going to be with Tony or any other white boy. She's too—"

"I'm too what?" I probe.

"Too . . . I don't know, I can't find the word," Nikki says. "But it just seems like, well, relationships—no matter how good they are and what the people have in common—are difficult. So why make it more complicated?" Nikki asks.

Essence agrees. "Yeah, I couldn't do it. I wouldn't want to be constantly having to explain my culture."

"So then, we should just stay in our bubble and not get to know anyone else?" I ask.

Nikki crosses her legs. "That's not what we're saying."

"Well, what are you saying?" I am so torn right now. I agree with them. I do. But I disagree, too.

Essence says, "You know, I guess it just comes down to what your type is. I just ain't never liked no white boy. Don't think I ever will. But I will admit it, Tony is cute," she says. "For a white boy."

"That's kind of messed up, Essence," I say. "You act like Tony is an exception to some rule. What if someone said you were cute for a black girl?"

Essence picks up a magazine from the table next to my bed and flips through it. "Okay, you're right. I didn't mean it like that. I'm just saying, *I've* never been attracted to a white guy. I mean, yes, there are plenty of cute ones. Tony happens to be the cutest *I've* met," she explains. "But I really do think it's about what you want. I mean, let's take race out of it," she says. "What if a guy had only three teeth, was missing two fingers, and walked around with a neck twitch. Would you date him?"

Nikki and I burst into laughter. We are laughing so loud, Mom calls out to us and tells us to quiet down.

"But really," Essence says. "It wouldn't matter how nice he was. You wouldn't date him because that's not the type of guy you prefer. We all have our list—whether we admit it or not—of our ideal person. All I'm saying is, a white guy has never been on my list."

I play with my hair and reach for the rubber band that's wrapped around my bedpost. "You've got a point," I say. "I guess it's complicated. I mean, keeping race out of it, what if you like someone, love him, even, but more like a deep friendship. You know? And then there's someone else that makes you feel things you've never felt. Makes you—"

Nikki gets up from my bed and slides her feet into her slippers. "Is this hypothetical?" She looks at me with her twin vision, trying to read me.

"Just a question," I say.

"Well," she says. "I think feelings come and go. Sometimes you have to go with logic. I mean, if you have a deep friendship with someone, why give that up? Friendships make relationships stronger. Look at Mom and Dad."

"High school sweethearts, just like Malachi and me," Essence says.

"Mom is always talking about how she chose to love Dad. It wasn't about the butterflies at first but they came."

"Right," I say.

Nikki walks to the door. "I'm going to the kitchen to get something to drink. Want anything?" she asks us.

Essence and I say no.

Nikki turns and looks at me again. "Hypothetical question, right?"

"Right."

When she comes back to the room, she has a menu in her hand. "Want to order a pizza?"

"I don't have any money for that," Essence says.

"I got you," Nikki and I say at the same time.

Nikki and Essence go back and forth about what kind of pizza to get. I lie down on top of the covers and close my eyes.

Why did I hesitate to answer their question about Tony? Why do I get that feeling every time someone mentions his name, or when his eyes look into mine?

Nikki picks the phone up to dial for delivery. “Maya, do you know what you want?”

I thought I did.

CHAPTER 30

The next morning, Nikki's alarm goes off, and she doesn't even budge. She is asleep in my bed, and Essence is on the air mattress. I get out of bed and go across the hallway to Nikki's room. Her alarm gets louder the closer I get to it. I turn it off and lie on her bed. I don't even know if I'll be able to get back to sleep. I look at the stuff she has spread across her end table and see two college brochures. One from the University of Oregon and the other, Washington State. Just when I pick them up, Nikki is standing at the door. "Why are you in my bed?"

"You're not going to Spelman?"

Nikki rubs her eyes and snatches the brochures from me. "Why are you in my room?"

"Both you and Essence are just going to go to other schools like we haven't planned this?"

Nikki puts the catalogs on her dresser. "I just want to explore other options," she says. "Ms. Bryant says it's a good idea to apply to several schools."

"Right, but U of O? Washington State? We've always said we'd go to a historical black college."

Nikki doesn't say anything.

It's one thing for me to think of not having Essence with me in college. But Nikki? How can I exist without my sister by my side? I don't even know how to think about what my life would be like if I didn't have her close to me.

"I am not saying I don't want to go to Spelman. I am just applying to other schools, too."

"But why didn't you tell me?" I ask.

"Do I have to tell you everything?" Nikki says.

I open my mouth to answer, but then I just get up, go back to my room.

No. We don't have to tell each other everything.

CHAPTER 31

Snow is still on the ground but the beauty of it has melted into dingy slush. I meet Charles and Star at Tony's house for another meeting. After Charles and Star leave, Tony asks me if I want to stay so we can watch his Alfred Hitchcock collection.

We walk downstairs into the basement, which is no longer a creepy dungeon but a game lounge. There's a pool table and dartboard, and framed play-bills and movie posters are hanging on the wall. On the other side of the basement, there's a sofa and two armchairs.

We sit on the sofa.

"Whose turn is it?" Tony asks. Another game of questions is about to begin. Tony and I have made this our ritual every time we're together.

"It's your turn," I say.

"You sure?" He leans back on the sofa and stretches his legs out.

I realize how close we are sitting, and I get a tidal wave in my stomach. "I'm positive. It's your turn."

"Okay, here's my question," Tony says. Then he asks, "Do you know how much I like you?" He says this as if he's asking me what time it is.

I can't even open my mouth to answer.

"I'll take that as a no," he says. "Well, I do. And I have since the first day we talked." Tony turns to me, scoots even closer to me so there is no space between us. "I know it's your turn," he says. "But can I ask another question?"

I still can't speak.

"Do you like me as much as I like you?"

What happened to questions about favorites and hobbies? I guess we're past that.

"I can't," I say in a soft whisper. "I can't."

Tony scoots back. "You and Devin don't seem—"

"We've known each other our entire lives," I tell him.

"You didn't answer my question. I asked you if you liked me as much as I like you."

I know I didn't answer his question, but I feel like he needs to understand that with Devin there's history.

Tony starts laughing. "I've never seen you speechless. You always—*always*—have something to say."

I smile. And even though I know the answer to his question, I just can't bring myself to answer him.

Tony puts the DVD in and hits the Play button. "I'll let it go . . . for now," he says.

I can't believe this is happening. I can't believe how happy I am that it is.

We must watch five episodes and just as the credits roll, I blurt out, "I don't like him." It's a declaration. "I don't." The second time I say it, I believe myself even more.

"Then why did you say you can't?" Tony is trying to sound neutral, like before. But I can hear a twinge of frustration in his voice. Frustration or maybe sadness. Sometimes they sound the same.

"I—it's just how it's supposed to be," I tell Tony. And then, as if the words can't help themselves from spilling out of my mouth, I say, "I'm not supposed to like you." I cover my mouth quickly and gasp, trying to inhale the words back in but it's too late. "What I meant was—"

"Because I'm white?"

"No. I-I didn't mean that." I get choked on my words. They are tangled and twisted on my tongue and nothing is coming out right. I take a deep breath. My tongue betrays me again, and before I can tell it not to, it says, "Tony, I like you. Okay? I like you a lot. Even though I don't want to."

"You don't want to like me? What does that mean?"

Now no words will come.

"If I like you and you like me, what's the problem?"

There is no easy answer to his question.

"It's not the fifties, you know." Tony takes my hand. And those feelings return, my hiccuping heart, the tidal waves in my belly. This time I don't push them away. Instead, when his lips touch mine, I kiss them back. Tony's fingers play in my hair. The skinny twists wrap around his fingers. Has he ever touched a black girl's hair? How do I feel in his hand?

The basement is lit by a lamp in the corner. Upstairs, I can hear footsteps walking in and out of rooms. I back away from Tony. "What if your mom comes down here?"

"She won't." Tony continues kissing me.

"What about your dad?"

"He won't." Tony pulls me closer to him.

I have lost time. Kissing Tony starts and stops and starts again until we fall asleep in each other's arms.

Hours have passed, and the only reason I wake up is because I hear noise upstairs. Footsteps walking again, and then a voice. "Tony? Are you down there?"

Tony's dad is standing at the doorstep. Tony jumps up. "Uh, yeah, I'm . . . yeah. Watching TV still."

My blurry eyes adjust on the digital clock. It's midnight.

"Just checking." Tony's dad doesn't walk away. I can feel him standing there at the top of the stairs. Tony and I stay still. I try not to breathe too hard. A few minutes pass, and Mr. Jacobs closes the door and walks away.

Tony gets up from the sofa. "I, uh, you should get home," he says. He takes his arm from around me and gets up. "Sorry. Didn't mean to keep you here so late."

I am already getting my story together for Mom and Dad. I'll tell them I was with Essence, that Malachi dropped me off. I get my stuff together and follow Tony upstairs. Instead of walking up both flights of stairs, Tony stops at the back door and opens it. "I'll walk you across the street," he whispers.

"That's okay. I'm fine."

He gives me his "are you sure?" look.

"Really. I'm fine."

Tony kisses me once more. Soft.

As soon as I step outside, the cold hits me and what happened tonight feels exposed. My feet crunch the snow as I walk from his backyard to the front. The streetlights create shadows on the leftover snow, and I can tell that a cat has walked this way. His paw prints create a path toward my driveway. I cross the street.

I tiptoe in my house and make it to bed without waking anyone. Once I'm in bed, I am wide awake. All I can think about is Tony, his lips, our kiss. And I feel really silly admitting this, but as I wait to fall asleep, I whisper his name over and over.

Tony Jacobs.

Tony Jacobs.

Tony Jacobs.

And I like how the *n* kisses the roof of my mouth. How my lips open wide to pronounce the *o*. His name is a sweet lullaby.

Tony Jacobs.

Tony Jacobs.

Tony Jacobs.

CHAPTER 32

I'm supposed to see Essence today. On my way to the bus stop, I walk past Devin's block. I stand on the corner, knowing I need to turn right, walk to his house, tell him. But before I do that, I stand a bit longer. It is raining, and the slushy snow that was piled at the curb is dissolving even more. I breathe in, out, turn right.

Devin lives on a dead-end street. Cars accidentally turn onto this block, and the drivers soon realize they can't get where they want to go. It is a street of mistakes, a disappointment. His house is at the end of the block, hidden behind untamed bushes. The grass is stiff. Even though there's a gate around his house, the latch is broken, so I just walk up to the porch and knock on the door because the doorbell doesn't work.

I knock a few more times but no one comes to the door. And I know it's the cowardly thing to do but I go into my purse and take out a piece of paper. Yes, I could call or wait until I see Devin face-to-face, but this is easier. I write him a letter, telling him that I can't be in a relationship with him. I leave out the part about me thinking we don't have much in common other than being black and growing up in the same neighborhood. I leave out the part about having so much fun with Tony, about how we laugh and how we both are motivated to make a difference at Richmond. And I definitely don't tell him about the kiss. For all Devin knows, I'm busy with school and college applications and I just don't have time. He'll understand that.

I fold the paper, put his name on it, and slide it in his mailbox. A car drives onto the street. I think maybe it is his aunt coming home. But I am wrong. The car pulls into the driveway and backs up, turning around so it can go back to Jackson Avenue.

I walk away, leaving this dead-end street.

On the bus, halfway to Essence's house, my phone vibrates in my pocket. I take it out, see Devin's name flashing on the screen. I don't answer.

CHAPTER 33

I am in the den when the doorbell rings. Dad calls out, "I got it!" So I don't bother to get up. But then I hear Devin's voice, so I go to the door and crack it open, just enough so I can peek through to make sure it's him.

Just as I'm about to close the door and hide, Mom sees me. "Devin's here," she says. "Your dad is finally finishing my sewing room today. They're painting the walls."

"Oh, uh, that's, that's good. 'Bout time, huh?" I haven't told anyone that I broke up with Devin. This probably isn't a good time.

Mom looks at me like she's trying to figure something out. "You're not going to come and say hello? I hear he has good news."

I come out and walk with Mom to the kitchen. Dad is smiling so hard, I am sure his cheeks will hurt later. He kisses me on my forehead. "I can't believe you kept this from me, Maya."

I look at Devin.

Devin stutters, "Oh, uh—no, she, I didn't tell her yet."

Dad steps back, looks at both of us. "Sorry I ruined the surprise."

Devin says, "It's okay." He looks down at the floor.

Mom looks at me, her face confused. "Well, aren't you going to congratulate him? It's not every day a student gets a full ride to Morehouse College."

I don't even realize the tear rolling down my cheek until she hands me a napkin. I hear her whisper to Dad that they should leave, and when they do, I reach out to Devin, take his hand. He pulls me into himself and we hug. Tight. "I'm so proud of you," I whisper. "And I'm so sorry I—I still care, I just—"

Devin wipes my tears. "Don't apologize. I get it."

"You do?"

"Yeah, I mean, I'm busy with school, too. Senior year is hectic," he says. "But maybe we can try it again in Atlanta."

I don't know if I should ruin this moment for him. It's not fair to make this about me, about us, when really it should be about him accomplishing the thing he worked so hard for.

Devin knows me, though, and so he steps back and says, “It’s not about school. We’re not getting back together, are we?”

“No,” I admit. “I’m sorry, Devin. I should’ve been honest with you. I just, I never wanted to hurt you. I wanted to stick to our plan.” I feel like I’m just babbling, so I stop talking. Then I take a deep breath and say what I think I’ve been feeling this whole time. “Devin, I think I wanted to be with you because everyone else wanted me to be. But really, you’re my friend—in every sense of the word. We’re like—”

“Like best friends?”

“Yes,” I answer.

“Always?”

“Always.”

CHAPTER 34

Christmas is in three days. Tony and I meet outside in front of my house and walk over to Jackson Avenue. He is shopping for Kate. It is cold today, December cold. No rain, no sun. Just an ordinary gray day. The shops along Jackson Avenue are decorated with Christmas lights, and the sidewalks are full of shoppers walking in and out of the boutiques.

There are cars parked at every inch of the curb, even on the side streets. I don't know if I will ever get used to my neighborhood being the place where people flock *to* instead of flee from.

Tony takes my hand. This is the first time we've been out together since I broke up with Devin. When we turn the corner, I see Tasha and Cynthia sitting in Daily Blend. I don't even think about what I'm doing or why, I just slip my hand out of Tony's, rub my hands together, and put them in my pocket, pretending to be cold.

I hate myself for this.

"It's your turn," Tony says. "What's your question?"

I have a question. But I don't ask it out loud.

CHAPTER 35

Star and Charles have been camped out with me all day at Tony's again. I think Charles is onto me and Tony, but he doesn't say anything. When they leave, Tony says, "I have something for you." He runs upstairs, then comes back down with brochures in his hands. "Okay, so before I give you these, just know that I'm not against Spelman. I just care about you, and I want to make sure you're making the best decision."

When he hands me the brochures, I realize they are college catalogs.

"These are the top journalism schools in the country," Tony says. "I know your dream is to write for a big-time paper or magazine, so I just thought, well, I just don't want you to sell yourself short."

I bite my lip, try to hear him out.

"I mean, Columbia University is the top ranked—"

"Tony, I know that. But that's not the point," I tell him. "And isn't it too late to apply?"

"You have till January first."

"Wow, you actually checked?" I set the brochures down on the coffee table. "It's more complicated than just choosing based on rank, Tony. You wouldn't understand."

"Don't just tell me I wouldn't understand. Explain it to me," Tony says. "Why Spelman?"

"Because at Spelman, I'd learn about black history in a way that I just can't get anywhere else," I explain. "And for once—for once!—being a black woman who is successful will be the norm, and I'll have plenty examples of strong black women right in front of me."

The more I think about it, the more excited I get.

"Because my grandmother and mother went there. Because it was founded on the belief that every black girl deserves to be accepted and educated. Because it has produced thousands of successful black women. And because, because it's not just Spelman, it's Atlanta. There are all kinds of blacks there. I want to live in a place where there's a variety of black people, doing all kinds of things. I've never had that. You get to see and experience all kinds of white people all the time."

I stop talking because I don't think I'm doing Spelman justice. "I can't articulate all my reasons, Tony, but, well, let me ask you this. Did you look up anything about Spelman? Or did you just think since you've never heard of the school it must not be worth going to?"

"Maya, that's not fair—"

"Did you know that Spelman produces Fulbright Scholars consistently? That it's one of the top-ten female universities?"

"I'm not saying it's not a good school, I was just wondering if it's the best school given your goals."

I look through the rest of the brochures. Just about all of them have mostly white people on the cover smiling or posing as if in deep thought, with a few token people of color in the photo, too. I put them on the table. "Well, it might not be the best for journalism, but it's the best for me," I say.

"I get it, I think. I mean, I don't know what it feels like, but I understand why it's important to you."

Tony is sitting on the edge of the sofa.

We don't talk for a while and then Tony says, "Sorry, Maya. I didn't mean to offend you."

"No, don't. Don't apologize. I'm actually glad we can hear each other out. One of my fears about dating you was that we wouldn't be able to have honest conversations. Thank you for, for listening."

Tony scoots back on the sofa. Gets comfortable and turns the TV on.

The front door opens. Tony sits up, takes his arm from around me.

"We're home," Mrs. Jacobs calls out. Mr. Jacobs is behind her, carrying two tote bags full of groceries. Mrs. Jacobs smiles at me. "Hi, Nikki. How are you?"

"Mom, this is Maya," Tony says.

Mrs. Jacobs looks at me. "I'm so sorry. Forgive me."

"It's okay."

Mr. Jacobs mumbles a hello. He looks like the day has worn him out.

"What are you two up to?" Mrs. Jacobs unpacks the bags and puts the perishable food in the fridge.

Tony helps her. "Not much now. We were doing something for school, but now we're done."

"Would you like to stay for dinner, Maya?"

I look at Tony. "Stay," he says.

"Okay. Thank you."

"Sure. No problem at all," Mrs. Jacobs says.

Mrs. Jacobs takes out ground turkey from the bag. "Hope you like spaghetti."

"I do." I smile.

Mr. Jacobs goes to the fridge and grabs a beer. He cracks it open and comes into the living room and changes the station. "I haven't seen the news all day."

He flips channels and stops on a local station that is broadcasting live from a bank robbery. Mr. Jacobs turns the volume up. "Isn't this over by your school?" he says.

Tony comes back to the living room. "Yeah."

The reporter goes over the details. Customers and bank employees are being held hostage. Police cars surround the bank. The reporter looks into the camera and says, "We have reason to believe that there is more than one suspect in the bank."

Mrs. Jacobs whimpers. "Oh, no. Oh, God."

Tony picks up the remote. "This is depressing, Dad. Can I turn it?"

Mr. Jacobs says no.

The more the reporter says, the more anxious Mrs. Jacobs becomes. She is standing over the stove, cooking and praying. "Dear God, please don't let anyone get hurt. Please protect everyone in there."

The reporter standing outside the bank says, "We've just confirmed the identity of one of the suspects. He is believed to be—"

Oh, God, I think to myself. Please don't let him be black. Please.

I hold my breath.

Tony changes the channel before the anchorwoman finishes her sentence. "This is just going to drive you crazy, Mom," he says. "Let's watch something else." He flips through the stations.

Mr. Jacobs takes his beer and goes to his bedroom. "Let me know when dinner is ready, will you?"

I hate that the first thought that came to my mind was if the suspect was black. But ever since I was a child, I've carried the shame and pride of my black brothers and sisters. When a black person fails or succeeds it means something. All my life strangers have come up to Dad in a store, at the mall, or at church just to tell him how proud they are of him. "It's good to know that there's a good black man taking care of his family and doing something positive," they say. They never just call him a man. He is always a *black* man. I wonder, if he were white, would his accomplishments seem so significant?

I can't remember when I started to have these feelings of pride and shame. I guess they've always instinctively been there. From my earliest memories I remember feeling pride when a black person succeeded at something—anything. It was like part of me had succeeded, too. And if a black person failed, I felt embarrassed. Ashamed. Like when I'm on the bus and there's a group of black teens being loud and acting rowdy. I know white kids do this, too. I know whenever a big group is anywhere—a bus, a restaurant—they tend to act like it's just them, like they're in a bubble, like no one can hear them, like it doesn't matter how ridiculous they are being.

But it matters when it's a group of black teens.

I've seen the reaction from strangers. The fearful eyes, the irritated sighs, the way women clutch their purses, hold on tight. And sometimes I'm with the group. Sometimes I'm not. But all the time, if I catch it, if I catch the moment that one of them laughs too loud, or is being obnoxious and reciting explicit lyrics to a song they are listening to, I get embarrassed.

Do white people get that feeling?

CHAPTER 36

Once Christmas Eve came, Mom insisted on family time, so Nikki and I have been in the house mostly, or visiting our aunt's house. But now that Christmas is over, Mom is back at work and Nikki and I are back to doing what we want, which is mostly sleeping in.

It's noon and I am just waking up.

Nikki beat me to the shower, which is fine with me because I am in the perfect position in my bed and I don't feel like moving. The afternoon light is blocked out by my pulled-down shade. I get out of bed and step over the thick, lavender blanket that I must have kicked off while I was sleeping.

My blankets are always on the floor when I wake up. My pillow, too, sometimes. Mom says I'm the wild one, her fire child. "Must've been you kicking me so hard, twisting and turning in my womb," Mom's told me.

Nikki is Mom's rain. Refreshing and nourishing and everything good about rain. Not the thunderstorms or gloomy sky.

When we were younger, Nikki and I would get into our parent's bed in the middle of the night, scared from the boogie man or some noise we thought we heard. Dad would fuss, but Mom would let us stay in their king-size bed. We'd snuggle between them and fall right to sleep. By morning, all our bodies were intertwined. Feet in mouths, arms across bellies, heads at the foot of the bed.

I stumble my way to the bathroom, my eyes still caked with sleep. "Nikki, how much longer will you be?"

"Five minutes!"

I slide down the wall and sit on the floor.

The doorbell rings and I hear Dad say, "I think she's still asleep."

I stand and walk to the edge of the stairs.

"Maya?" Dad is at the foot of the steps. "Uh, Tony is here for you?" Dad says this as a question.

"He is? Oh, okay. I'm, I'm—"

"I'll tell him to wait down here for you," Dad says. "I'm gone to the center. Mom's at work."

"Okay."

Nikki comes out of the bathroom wrapped in a yellow towel. "Did I hear Dad say Tony is here?"

"Yeah."

"Another student council meeting?"

I have no idea why he's here. "Uh, yeah," I say. I go into the bathroom, close the door. I brush my teeth, wash my face, and go back to my room and try to find something decent to throw on so I can go downstairs to see what Tony wants.

Nikki knocks on my door and opens it at the same time. "Bye. I'm going over to Kate's."

I can't help but think of how ironic it is that Tony is here and Nikki is going over there. "Okay. Tell Tony I'll be down in a minute."

It definitely takes me longer than a minute. I change three times.

Once I am dressed, I do my hair. I put a small dab of coconut oil in my hand and rub it through my twists. I look into the mirror and see Tony standing in the doorway. "Can I come in?"

"Um, yes. What—what are you doing here?"

"I wanted to see you."

"Why didn't you call?"

"I don't know. I wanted to just stop by, I guess."

"Come in," I tell him. I walk over to the chair that's full of clean clothes—outfits I just put on and tossed. I move them to my bed. "Sit here."

Tony sits down.

I go back to my dresser, stand in front of the mirror. "I'm just doing my hair. I'm almost ready." I take the small bottle of oil in my hand and squirt a little onto my scalp.

Tony comes over to me. He picks up the bottle. "Smells good. What does this do?"

"It's hair oil. It keeps my scalp from getting too dry."

Tony takes the bottle, turns it upside down and puts a little oil in his hand. He puts his hand in my hair and massages my scalp. I close my eyes. His fingers slow dance with my twists; the palm of his hands press into my scalp, gentle, steady.

My hair must feel so unfamiliar in his hands. It is nothing like his mom's, or sister's, or any other girl's he dated before me. I look into the mirror and watch Tony, who is not looking at me. His eyes are studying my hair, each curl, each frizzy strand. He looks up, sees me in the mirror, and smiles. He kisses the back of my neck, kisses the spaces below each ear, and I am lost in him.

CHAPTER 37

I haven't seen Nikki much this week. She is always with Kate or Ronnie. I am always with Tony or Essence. But tonight, Mom makes sure our family is together to welcome in the New Year. This is one family commitment Dad never misses.

11:30 p.m.

Dad starts us off with our family tradition. We each share one thing we're thankful for and one resolution. Then we'll toast at midnight and drink sparkling apple cider. I don't really hear what anyone else has to say because while I'm waiting my turn, I am trying to think up an answer—well, I have answers, but none I can say out loud. Because if I told the truth, I'd say that I'm thankful for my relationship with Tony.

My resolution?

To tell the truth about us.

CHAPTER 38

School is back in session. It's lunchtime and I head to The Lounge to meet with Star, Charles, and Tony. Mrs. Armstrong leaves to go warm up her lunch. "Be right back," she says.

As soon as she leaves, I open my notebook. "I think we should invite the media to our school for our Black History Month assembly."

Charles leans forward in his chair. Tony is reading the press release that I scribbled. Mrs. Armstrong taught us the elements of a press release and the purpose they serve. I used her handout to help me draft my own.

I explain Richmond's annual Black History celebration to Tony. "Every February, we have a ceremony in the auditorium that is led by students."

Charles adds, "Sometimes students read poems by black poets. Last year I recited King's 'I Have a Dream' speech."

Star says, "And Maya always sings. Last year, she was amazing." She smiles at me. "So amazing."

Tony looks at me. "Yeah, I hear Maya can sing. Can't say *I've heard* her sing, though."

I keep us on track. "The assembly is the only time we get to run the show. No adult does anything. It's all us." I continue, "So I think people should know about it. The news always wants to come to our school to report something bad, well, they should come see us at our best."

Charles leans back in his seat. "I don't know, Maya. I mean, I like the idea, but we need some kind of hook to get them here. What's really going to make the news come to Richmond?"

Tony is nodding, and his eyes roam in his head as he thinks up an answer.

And then I get an idea. "What if we find alumni who are doing something big and invite them to come speak or something?"

Charles leans forward. "That would be perfect."

Tony tells us, "St. Francis always had some former graduate visit our school to give us motivational talks."

Charles leans forward even more and says, “We could invite T. J. Downing.”

I start taking notes in my journal.

Star smiles. “God, the press would love that. Former Richmond point guard gives back to his community,” she says sarcastically. “Isn’t he playing overseas now?”

“Yeah. He was one of my dad’s mentees. They still keep in touch, and he comes home a lot,” I tell them.

A rainbow smiles across Charles’s face. “This is going to be good.”

CHAPTER 39

Principal Green says no.

"I've decided to have a diversity assembly take the place of our Black History Month celebration." His excuse for making this change is filled with words like "tolerance" and "unity." He tells us he has invited a guest speaker to come. "I appreciate your idea. I do, I really appreciate your idea," Principal Green says. "But inviting the media? No, no. Don't get me wrong, T. J. is a wonderful person. But he just reinforces what the community already knows about Richmond. They know our boys can play ball. I'd like us to focus on something else," he says. "And besides, we need to have an assembly that is for everyone, not just the black students."

"But black history *is* for everyone," I say.

Charles says, "And the assembly is a Richmond tradition."

Tony asks, "Why can't we celebrate both—diversity and black history?"

Star doesn't say anything. She is standing there chipping away at her nail polish.

Principal Green says his decision is final. "But I would like students to be involved. Maya, word around the school is that you can sing. Would you like to sing something at the assembly?"

"I, uh—"

Charles cuts me off. "With all due respect, sir, I think the rest of student council should have a say in this."

"Oh, your peers are all for it," Principal Green tells us. He hands me a sheet of paper. "Cynthia already made a flyer. She and a few others are hanging these up right now. You've got a great cabinet, Miss President."

I can't even get words to form on my tongue.

Star is the first to walk away, then Charles.

As soon as Tony and I step outside Principal Green's office, I hear yelling and cursing and Star's voice is the loudest. I turn the corner, and she is standing with crumpled flyers in her hands.

Cynthia is yelling, "You can't just rip our posters off the wall! Who do you think you are?"

"I think I've been at this school longer than you have and—"

"Are you telling me to go back to where I come from?" Cynthia yells. "You're such a racist—"

"Racist? I'm the one wanting to have a Black History Month celebration!" Star won't back down, and now there's a crowd forming. Nikki and Kate are with Essence, Malachi, and Ronnie. They walk over to me and stand with Charles and Tony.

Tasha stands next to Cynthia. Rachel, Joey, Vince, and Bags join them. And the more screaming and yelling Star and Cynthia do, the more people surround them.

Tasha blurts out, "Cynthia, don't let that white girl talk to you like that!"

And Cynthia acts all bad and bold and steps closer to Star like she's going to hit her.

Just then Principal Green appears. "That's enough! Enough."

The crowd disintegrates.

"Go to class, all of you, all of you!" Principal Green waits until everyone starts moving. He keeps an eye on Star and Cynthia, who go different directions. I am surprised he lets them go without calling them into his office.

I follow Star up the stairs. She pulls another flyer

off the wall. This time, a patch of paint comes with it. She turns to me and asks, "Are you going to help?"

I know that taking these flyers down won't do anything, but I join her. She takes down the ones on the left side of the hallway. I rip off the flyers on the right.

The tardy bell rings, but neither of us stops. I say, "How can he just change our tradition? And why is Cynthia such a kiss-up? When did she get to make all the decisions?"

After we've taken down most of the flyers, Star says, "I think celebrating diversity is fine, but not in the place of honoring black history. February is only twenty-eight days; they can at least give us that."

For the first time today I laugh.

The hallway is completely empty now except for the two of us. Star takes the last flyer off the wall and turns it over to its blank side. She takes a blue marker out of her bag and writes WE DESERVE 28 DAYS. She refolds the ball of tape and sticks it on the back of the flyer. "They can't just change things like that." She looks around and discreetly hangs the flyer on the wall. It's crooked and the tape is so weak that it's barely hanging.

I am regretting that I am just now getting to know Star.

I slip into Mr. Anderson's calculus class, and he doesn't even notice that I'm late. I try to focus on the assignment, but I can't fully get my mind off Principal Green and Cynthia, and the fact that I'm a president with no power.

The bell rings just as I finally zone in to get some work done. I have almost forgotten about the flyer Star wrote on, but when I get back in the hallway I see papers of all different sizes and colors taped to the wall. The handwriting is different on each sheet of paper:

PUT BLACK BACK IN HISTORY.

CELEBRATE EVERYONE!

GO BACK TO THE HILLS.

THIS IS OUR SCHOOL, TOO!

WHO CARES?

And the one that's making Principal Green curse:

The words *Black History* with a drawing of a fried chicken leg and a slice of watermelon under it.

"What in the world is going on here?" Principal Green is yelling in the hallway and pulling the self-made posters off the walls. "If anyone knows who did this, you must let a staff member know. Anything hung on school property without prior permission is considered vandalism."

No one is saying anything. He takes down the poster Star hung. "Who started this?" he asks. No one answers. “Well, I’m finishing it. Be aware that anyone who hangs anything up without permission will have detention and possible suspension.”

The two-minute bell rings. We unfreeze and make our way to our next class. As I walk down the hall, I see that Principal Green missed one. It says “Celebrate Tradition.”

I don’t take it down.

CHAPTER 40

We've spent most of class working on our final drafts for the next issue of the *Richmond Reporter*. There's about ten minutes left until lunch. Mrs. Armstrong walks to the front of the room and says, "All right, everyone, before you get out of here I need to give you your homework assignment."

I take out something to write with and open my notebook.

Mrs. Armstrong takes the cap off a dry-erase marker and begins writing a list on the board.

Samuel Cornish
John Brown Russwurm
Frederick Douglass
W. E. B. DuBois

Ida B. Wells
Ethel L. Payne
Nancy Hicks Maynard
Karl Fleming
Bernie Foster

Mrs. Armstrong turns around and snaps the top back on the pen. She leans against her desk, sitting on its edge. "These are names I want you to know. And I don't just want you to regurgitate information back to me. I want you to tell me why, out of all the people you could know, am I asking you to find out about them."

The bell rings and we rush to the door.

"I want photos, quotes, facts. Who are these people? Why should we know them?" Mrs. Armstrong says.

I know I could work on this tonight when I get home, but I'm curious to know who these people are. I mean, I know who Fredrick Douglass is. I know that he was a former slave who started a black antislavery newspaper called *The North Star*. I'm assuming that the rest of the people on the list have something to do with journalism.

I go to the library and ask Mrs. Butler if I can use the computer. "I've got some research to do," I tell her.

"On the computer?" she asks. "I expect more thorough research from you."

"It's just to get me started," I say.

Mrs. Butler smiles.

I sit down at a computer and randomly pick a name off the list.

CHAPTER 41

Ethel L. Payne.

She was known as the First Lady of the Black Press and gave a voice to the civil rights movement by writing articles about the Montgomery Bus Boycott; the desegregation of a high school in Little Rock, Arkansas; the protests in Birmingham and Selma, Alabama; and the March on Washington in 1963. In 1973 when she took the job as a commentator for CBS, she became the first black woman to become employed by a national broadcast.

I scribble these facts in my notebook.

I can hear Mrs. Armstrong saying, "Don't just tell me what. Tell me why."

Nothing is ever simple with Mrs. Armstrong, so it

has to be more than just the fact that Ethel L. Payne was a journalist.

I read over my notes, look for the answer.

CHAPTER 42

I walk out of the library armed with my notes on Ethel L. Payne and the extra articles about her that Mrs. Butler let me print. After begging with her, she even let me print a photo.

There's about ten minutes of lunch left, so I make my way to the cafeteria to get a bag of chips out of the vending machine.

I see Star walking toward me. "There you are. I just asked Nikki if she knew where you were."

"Library," I say. "Got an early start on some homework." I hold up the picture of Ethel L. Payne. Under her photo, there's a short bio about her.

We walk down the quiet hallway. Star sighs. "Are you going—" She stops in the middle of her sentence and starts a new one. "Do you see that?" Star stops walking and stands in front of a sign hanging on the wall.

WE ALREADY KNOW YOUR HISTORY

"Seriously? Who is putting up these ridiculous posters?" Star reaches to take it down.

I grab her hand. "Don't," I tell her. I look around to see if anyone is looking. I think I hear footsteps, but then no one comes, so I hold up the printout and say, "Let's put this one up right next to it."

Star hesitates, then smiles. She looks around, too, and then says, "Hold on." She eases the sign off the wall and tears the tape in half. "Here we go." Star takes my printout and hangs it on the wall next to the poster. Then she reaches into her bag and takes out a pen.

"What are you doing?"

Star doesn't answer me. She just starts writing.

DO YOU KNOW HER?

I hear footsteps and voices.

Star and I run down the hall.

The bell rings and students flood out of the cafeteria.

We blend in and walk with them to our next class, trying to catch our breath, our chests rising and rising.

CHAPTER 43

It looks too dark to be only three-thirty in the afternoon. Rain must be coming. I'm so glad Tony drove to school today. "So are you going to sing at the assembly?" Tony asks.

I'm in the backseat next to Nikki. Kate is in the front. Kate turns and looks at me. "That would be so cool if you sang. I hear you and Nikki both can sing really well."

"I'm not singing at that assembly," I tell them.

Nikki shakes her head in disappointment. "What, are you going to boycott again?"

"You can sing," I say.

"Principal Green didn't ask me to sing. He asked you."

"He won't care what token black girl sings the

black national anthem. He just wants something that represents us colored folk." I laugh. Tony looks like he wants to laugh, too. But he doesn't.

Kate doesn't seem to know what to do. "Are you really the only black person on the program?"

"Well, I'm not on the program. But, yes, pretty much. He's having representatives from each culture or race, or whatever he wants to call it, on the program. It feels, I don't know, it feels—"

"Forced?" Kate asks.

"Exactly."

Nikki shakes her head again.

And I can't believe that Kate seems to get it more than she does.

"I just want to hear you sing," Tony says. "So since you're not going to perform at the assembly, how about we get a song right now." He looks at me through the rearview mirror.

I look at Nikki. "Only if you sing with me," I say.

Nikki says, "Okay. I'll sing."

Tony's eyes get happy, and Kate sits up straighter in her seat.

Nikki and I count off and then we serenade them with the song we always sing when people put us on the spot. "A-B-C-D-E-F-G—"

Tony and Kate laugh. Tony says, "That's so wrong. So very wrong."

"But I have to say, if you sound this good singing the ABCs, I can't imagine how good you really are," Kate says.

Tony turns on the radio. "Guess we'll have to listen to this, since we can't get any live music," he says. "Just promise me that I'll get to hear you really sing one day." He looks at me again and I almost answer him, promise him, but then I feel Nikki looking at us, picking up our vibe with her twin sister magic.

I don't say anything. I look out the window, watch the changing sky.

CHAPTER 44

The poster war has been going on for a week. Star and I had no idea one little sign would cause all this drama. I guess in a way we started it, but we have no idea who's keeping it going. The dismissal bell rings, releasing us for the weekend. It's Friday, and even the teachers seem eager to get out of here.

On my way to my locker I see students standing around the poster of Ethel L. Payne. Principal Green is standing in the middle of the mob yelling, "Who did this? Who did this?"

I strain to see the poster. Someone has marked up Ethel's face, and on the borders of the poster the words *fat* and *ugly* are written over and over.

Vince calls out, "He did it! I saw him." He points

to Devin, who is holding a black Sharpie in his hand, along with poster board paper.

"This is for my presentation!" Devin shouts. He throws the oversize paper down and reaches into his bag. He pulls out a handout from our science class. "See, we have to make a poster about—"

"I saw him do it!" Vince repeats.

Devin yells back at him, and they start cursing at each other over who's lying. Then Principal Green tells Devin, "Come with me."

"For what? I didn't do anything! How are you going to take his word over mine?"

The yelling and cursing is contagious. Students scream at Principal Green and at one another, taking sides. It's too loud to make out what anyone is saying, but over all the hollering, one word cuts through the noise.

"Nigger!"

I don't know whose lips spewed the word, but I know it came from behind me. When I turn around, Bags, Joey, Vince, and Tony are standing there, the four of them looking around like they're trying to find out who said it.

I have heard that word before. Mostly in documentaries about the civil rights movement. This is the first time I've heard the word in real life. The first time the *er* is at the end. Pronounced clearly and precise enough to cut. This is the first time it's been said in my presence to communicate hate.

I've heard it on my block when boys greet each other, when the *er* is replaced by an *a*. When it's a word of solidarity and brotherhood. I've heard it in lyrics when it's a word of pride, when it's a word black people have taken back, taken the negative power of it and reshaped it into something good. But Dad says it was never our word so it's not something we can take back. He says it will always symbolize a beaten slave, a hanging noose, a burning cross.

That word hangs in the hallway like black men's bodies hung from trees. It lingers and struggles and chokes out all the air. It is a word that suffocates. It is a word that makes me see Confederate flags and a bloated Emmett Till sinking in dirty water.

I feel hot all over. Angry tears fight their way down my face, falling slow and reluctantly. I have to get out of here. I turn around to leave and see Tasha walking over to Tony.

"I know you didn't just say what I think you said!" Tasha shouts. She gets in Tony's face.

"What? That wasn't me! I didn't, I—"

"Everybody settle down right now. Right now!" Principal Green stands between Tasha and Tony.

"Everyone out of the building. Everyone. It's time to go home," Principal Green says. He looks at Devin. "Young man, you make your way to my office."

"He ain't got to go to your office?" Tasha asks, staring at Tony.

"Out of the building now!" Principal Green says.

All the commotion has brought other teachers to the hallway. Just as they start moving everyone toward the exit, Devin barges through the crowd. "I'm not going to your office if they don't have to go." He points to Vince, Bags, Joey, and Tony. "I'm going home. I didn't do anything."

"Devin! Devin!" Principal Green is not going to win. Devin walks out the door.

Students are still standing in the hallway, yelling and telling each other what just happened, as if we all didn't just experience it.

"Did you see that?"

"I know he wrote it!"

"I heard him say it."

"Principal Green is a sellout."

Tony grabs my hand. "Let's get out of here," he says.

I snatch my hand from his grasp.

"I think we should go," he says.

"I'm coming," I yell over the noise. I follow him,

walking through the crowd, forging my way, bumping up against backpacks, squeezing myself through the groups who refuse to move.

Teachers start ushering us out one door, not letting anyone go anywhere except outside. "And go home. Don't loiter around the building," a teacher says.

"Come on, move it along," another teacher calls out. "This way, this way." He holds a door open and calls us toward him with his hand.

Tony and I walk outside. He is walking so fast in front of me, I can barely keep up. The sidewalk is crowded. We cross the street and wait for Nikki and Kate to come out. "You didn't want to hold my hand?" Tony yells. I've never heard him yell before.

"Tony, did you see what just happened in there? I mean, really, are you crazy or something? This is not the time for holding hands." I look for Nikki and Kate. No sign of them.

"Have you told your friends about us?" he asks. Still yelling.

"Tony, stop making a scene," I say.

"Have you told *anyone*? Nikki? Essence? Anyone?"

"This is not the time or place to talk about it."

"Are you ashamed of us?"

"Tony, stop yelling at me and stop asking me questions."

"No. I want you to answer me. Why wouldn't you hold my hand?"

"I didn't want—"

"People to know we're together?"

"Do you really think it's a good idea to take my hand after what you've been accused of?"

"I didn't say it!"

"That's not the point. My point is our relationship is not some kind of statement. I didn't want to bring attention to the two of us. I don't want drama."

"Well, if Devin hadn't vandalized the school there wouldn't have been—"

"He didn't do it."

"Common sense says the person holding the marker is the one who wrote on the wall!"

Most students clear out and make their way home by foot or bus. Tasha comes outside and leans against the school wall. I wonder who she is waiting for and why she is staring at me. She doesn't even care that I see her looking. It's almost like she wants me to say something to her, but instead I just keep talking to Tony.

"Look, Devin didn't do it. I know him," I repeat.

"You don't know everything about him," Tony says.

"I know him better than I know you."

My words sting Tony's eyes. "What are you saying? You don't, you don't believe me?"

"I'm saying I believe you both."

"Are you? Because you have to know I would never—"

"I know."

Nikki and Kate finally come out of the building. I see Tasha say something to Nikki before they cross the street.

On our way walking home, Tony is walking ahead of us all, and Kate is quietly trailing behind him. Nikki and I are walking side by side. I say to Nikki, real low, "What did Tasha say to you?"

She makes sure Kate and Tony can't hear her, then says, "Blood is thicker than water."

CHAPTER 45

All the drama at school hasn't dampened our excitement for the winter formal, which is Valentine's Day weekend. We have two weeks to get our dresses. Somehow Nikki convinced Mom to let us use the car so we could go shopping. I don't know what I'm most nervous about, telling everyone who I am going to the dance with or riding in a car that Nikki is driving.

I am making my bed when Nikki comes into my room, without knocking, as always. She says, "You know it's not too late. Devin hasn't asked anyone else."

I fluff my pillows and toss them at the head of the bed. "I have a date," I say.

"Whatever," Nikki says. Then when she sees I'm not laughing, she yells, "Who?"

"I'll tell you later, when Essence gets here."

Mom gave Essence money for a dress, so we decided to all go shopping together.

"Why can't I know now?"

"Because I want to have the conversation only once." I leave my room and walk downstairs.

Nikki follows me, running down the steps. "Who? Charles and Tony are the only guys you hang with, and I know it's not one of them."

I ignore her comment and say, "I'll tell you when Essence gets here."

Why did I even bring it up? Guess I needed to get myself ready. This way, there's no backing out. Nikki is not going to let it go. And besides that, I'm tired of hiding our relationship. I didn't mean for it to go on this long. Seems like there just hasn't been a good time to say something.

The doorbell rings.

"I'll get it," Nikki says. "It's probably Kate."

"Kate's coming?"

"Yeah, I invited her. She hasn't found a dress yet."

I wanted to talk with Nikki and Essence today. Just the three of us. I can't say anything about Tony now.

Once Essence gets here, we leave. As soon as we back out of the driveway, Nikki says, "Okay, so who's this guy you're going to prom with?"

"We'll talk about that later," I say.

"Maya," Nikki whines.

"She's going with Devin," Essence says. "I don't even know why we're having this discussion."

"We'll talk about it later," I tell them. I don't want to make Kate feel awkward.

Kate changes the subject—I think maybe to save us both. "I love it downtown," she says. "Look at all the characters here."

We drive past Pioneer Square, the part of town everyone calls Portland's living room. Every type of person is hanging out in the square today—girls with hair the colors of a kaleidoscope, parents on playdates with their children, businesspeople on their lunch breaks, teens skateboarding—everyone fits here.

I remember the walks I used to take with Dad through this square. The bricks have names on them, and I felt bad for stepping on people's names. I always wondered how a person got to have his name on a brick. I still don't have an answer, but I'm sure ordinary people don't get to have their names here.

It takes us forever to find parking, and once we do it takes even longer for Nikki to parallel park. The four of us go inside a small shop that Kate swears has the best formal dresses and begin our search.

It doesn't take long for Essence and me to decide. She chooses a grayish-blue strapless dress that falls to the floor in the most elegant way. I'm wearing black. I found a dress that hits right at the knee and flares out. There's a turquoise sash that can be tied around my waist in lots of different ways. It's simple but stylish. Fits me perfectly.

Essence and I take our dresses to the counter and pay for them. Then we plop down in the soft armchairs in the waiting area of the dressing room. Nikki and Kate are trying on everything in the store. The clerk has brought them all kinds of dresses and sometimes the same dress in a different color or size.

"So, Maya," Nikki calls out from her dressing room. "Are you just messing with us or are you really not going with Devin?"

Essence answers for me. "They're going. I mean, okay, they're not dating anymore, but they can still—"

"Can we please stop talking about this?" I say.

Essence can't stop. "I'm just saying. We've planned out our whole senior year and—"

"And you're talking about *not* going to Spelman, remember?"

Nikki comes to Essence's rescue. "Maya, that's so different."

I concede. "Can we please just talk about this later?"

"Fine," Nikki says. I can see her feet stepping

into a gown. I hope she likes this one. I'm hungry and ready to get something to eat.

Finally, Kate and Nikki come out together for their big reveal. Kate's dress is the color of a pomegranate; Nikki's, the inside of a peach. They stand in the full-length, four-way mirror and look themselves over.

"I think these are the ones," Essence says.

Nikki asks, "You guys don't think it's too tight?" She turns around so we can see how it fits over her butt.

"No, girl, Ronnie will like that," Essence says.

Kate agrees. "You look good." She stands sideways so she can see her figure in the mirrors that are in front of us. "I wish I could fill out a dress like that." She pats her flat butt and laughs. "It's really pathetic back there, isn't it?"

Essence looks her over. "Big butts aren't everything. And, girl, your front definitely makes up for it."

We all laugh as Kate covers her breasts, as if they're bare. "They've always been big. I hate that." Then Kate holds her hair in her hand as if she's going to put it in a ponytail. But she has no hair tie. She swings it from side to side. "And this hair. Ugh! It's unstyleable. It can't hold curls or do anything but hang flat." She lets out a big sigh. "I need a makeover."

I never thought Kate would have these kind of insecurities.

Nikki takes one last look at herself in the mirror. "You sure it's okay?"

"Yes!" we all say at the same time.

"All right. I'm just not trying to look like a skank." Nikki goes back in her dressing room.

"You know I'm not going to let you go out looking a mess," I tell her. "People might think you're me."

We all laugh.

Nikki and Kate purchase their dresses, and we decide to get something to eat. Essence wants burgers from Red Robin, but when we get to thinking about the dresses we just bought, we decide to go the healthier route.

"How about Soul Food?" Nikki asks.

Essence says, "Ribs, greens, and mac and cheese are worse than a burger."

"Not that kind of soul food," Nikki explains. "It's—"

"Food that's good for your soul," Kate says.

"I don't want no rabbit food. I'm hungry," Essence says.

I agree.

Nikki promises us that if we're hungry afterward we'll get burgers. "Come on, just go once and if you don't like it, you don't have to go back. You two never want to try anything new."

"Let's go," I say.

Nikki looks surprised.

If she only knew all the new things I've been trying.

CHAPTER 46

Nikki pulls up to Soul Food. It is crowded, no parking spaces in the lot, so we park on the street.

As soon as Essence opens the menu she goes to criticizing everything. "Looks like all they got for me is water," she says.

"Try the edamame hummus," Nikki tells her. "It's actually good. I've had it before."

"You mean *that*?" I point to the table next to us, shaking my head in disgust. A glob of green in the middle of whole-grain tortilla chips.

"Just try it," Nikki says.

"Or what about those?" Kate points to a plate of food belonging to a man sitting at the same table as the hummus girl. There are three skewer sticks that have what looks like meat on them. "Those are vegan buffalo wings. Tastes just like chicken," she says.

"If you want to taste chicken, why don't you just eat chicken?" Essence asks. Loudly.

The man looks at us.

"No offense," Essence says.

He turns away.

I start laughing.

I pick up my glass of all-natural ginger ale. The pulp from the ginger has sunk to the bottom of the glass. I stir it with my straw and pass Essence the glass. "Here, taste this." She just about spits it out.

I think we'll be taking her to get a burger tonight.

"This is not soul food," Essence says. "They need to call the restaurant White Food!"

"Essence!" I can't believe she just said that. Out loud. In front of Kate.

"I'm just kidding." Essence laughs.

"No, you're not," Nikki says.

"Well, okay, I'm not," Essence says. "I mean, look who's up in here!" We all look around, and Essence, Nikki, and I are the only people of color in the entire restaurant.

We all get to laughing and can't stop. Kate is laughing, too, and it feels good to joke with her.

When the waitress comes, Essence says, "I'm

getting something I know," and orders pasta. I order a vegetable stir-fry with brown rice. Nikki and Kate order some fake meat dish and ask for two plates so they can split it.

When the food comes, everyone digs in and it must be good because none of us say anything for a while. Once Nikki is halfway through her soy barbeque chicken she looks at Kate and says, "So, Kate, are you and Roberto going to the winter formal together? Or are you going to bring someone from St. Francis?"

Kate hides her smile with her napkin, but her eyes are smiling, too. "Roberto," she says.

Essence gives a nod of approval, like she's a matchmaker. "Good choice," Essence says. "Who is Tony going to the dance with?"

It is definitely time to go.

I pick up the unpaid check and take money out of my purse so I can pay my half.

"I don't think Tony is going. He doesn't have a date," Kate says. "But who knows, he never talks about who he likes or who he's dating. I always find out through the girlfriend."

Well, she'll never know because I'm not saying anything.

Kate slurps the last of her iced tea. "My mom swears he's dating one of you," she says.

"Me?" Nikki and I say at the same time.

I almost choke on my ginger ale.

"Why me?" Nikki says.

"She swears she sees one of you and Tony together all the time at our house. But she can't tell you apart, so she can't say which one," Kate tells us. "I keep telling her you've only come over with me and that Maya has only been over for student council meetings with Star and Charles."

Kate looks at me, and my eyes drift quickly to the floor.

Nikki laughs. "That's so funny."

Kate's eyes won't give up. She is determined to make eye contact with me. "Yeah," she says. "I don't know where my mom gets her wacky ideas from," Kate says. "But I do think he's in love with someone. He's been acting weird lately."

I feel the left side of my mouth rise to a half smile, but I suppress it.

Essence asks, "So have your parents met Roberto yet?"

"Well, my mom met him once, but I'm probably not going to introduce him to my dad." Kate's eyes look down at the table, then at Nikki.

"Why not?" Essence asks.

Nikki starts making excuses. "It's not like they're boyfriend and girlfriend. Roberto only needs to meet

Mr. Jacobs if it gets serious. It's just one date." Nikki looks at Kate. "It's no big deal. Your dad doesn't even have to know." Nikki says this like she's said it before to Kate. "It's just a dance. Really. Just tell your dad you're coming with us."

"Why she gotta lie?" Essence asks. I kick her under the table.

Kate's voice gets real low. She looks around the restaurant and then leans in real close to the table. "My dad's from Canby. He just wasn't raised—he—"

Nikki finishes her sentence. "She doesn't think he'd be comfortable with her going out with someone who's Mexican."

I don't even think before I ask, "Well, what about Tony? Would your dad approve of Tony dating a black girl?"

Now Kate's eyes are avoiding mine.

CHAPTER 47

Student council has definitely become two separate teams. Charles, Star, Tony, and I are one team. Cynthia, Tasha, Rachel, and Joey are the other. Vince and Bags don't really count. Team One has started using our lunchtime to meet, but this morning Principal Green has called a meeting so he can check in with us about the scheduled activities coming up. We had to have it before school because just about all of us have an after-school class, club, or job to go to. Tony and I yawn our way into Richmond. "I have to stop at my locker," I say.

"Okay. I'll meet you in there."

I go to my locker and pull out another poster I put together. This one is of W. E. B. DuBois. Since no one is in the hall, this is a good time to hang it. I walk upstairs and find a spot. I take a roll of tape out of my bag and put the poster on the wall. Just as I smooth out the edges, push the corners against the wall really well, I hear footsteps.

Tap, tap.

Not *click*, or *squeak*.

These sound like nice shoes, like men's shoes. Not high heels, not sneakers.

I know I am in trouble.

I turn around, prepare myself to plead my case to Principal Green or some teacher who has caught me, but when I look up, Charles is standing there.

"It's you," he says.

I just stand there with the roll of tape dangling from my wrist.

Charles steps closer to me, reaches behind me, and says, "It's crooked." He straightens the poster, says, "There. That's better," and we walk away.

CHAPTER 48

The next morning Charles and I meet each other in a new spot. Charles says, "If Principal Green won't let us celebrate black history in the assembly, we'll celebrate it in the hallways."

I look at the poster he's made. It's a work of art. The name IDA B. WELLS is written at the top in a fancy font, and there's a photo of her on the left side. On the right side, there's a timeline of her life. "This is kind of amazing, Charles." Of course it would be. Charles wouldn't put out anything less.

Charles looks at his poster. "This woman was a journalist, an activist—she was, well, yeah, amazing. Her articles and pamphlets documented the unjust lynchings of the South and forced people to see what was going on. She was one of the founders of the

NAACP, and she fought for women's voting rights, as well as the rights for blacks to vote. I mean, what didn't she do?" Charles is talking fast and has his preacher man voice on.

I calm him down. "We better get out of here. You can't stand and admire your work. You have to hang fast and leave. Star and I almost got caught."

"Star?"

I start walking. "She's been helping me."

Charles and I walk together, slow and normal, like we didn't just defy Principal Green's rule. Charles says, "I have more made. I think we should put one up a day. I started researching and found some good ones—people that I think most of us don't know about."

Before we go our separate ways, Charles asks, "What about Tony?" And he looks at me like he's asking to know everything about Tony.

"He doesn't know about this," I say. And then I whisper really soft, as low as I can, "And no one knows about us."

Charles nods and walks to class.

CHAPTER 49

Mrs. Armstrong asks us to get into groups of three and tells us to discuss what we've learned about the people she assigned us. "I want you to focus your discussion on why you think I wanted you to know these people." I am with Essence and Tony. Mrs. Armstrong walks around the room listening in on our group for a moment before heading to the next group.

Tony starts the conversation off. "I didn't get to everyone on the list. But by the third person, I realized they were all black journalists, so I guess Mrs. Armstrong wanted to teach us this because it's Black History Month."

Essence looks through her notes. "But I think it's more than that. I think she wanted us to see how people fought to keep their stories being told. Every person on the list took a risk to tell the stories they felt needed to be shared."

I nod. "And not everyone on the list is black. Why didn't you look up everyone?" I try to ask the question without any judgment, but I can feel myself getting defensive. Tony always does his assignments. Why not this one?

"I don't know, I guess I felt like I got the point, so there was no need to look everyone up. I-I didn't think there was anyone white on the list."

Essence crosses her legs. "So you only want to learn about white journalists?"

"No, that's not what I'm saying. I just, I thought the point of the assignment was to learn about black writers because of Black History Month. So once I figured that out, I just moved on to my other homework. But, yes, I think it's important, and I get why we need to learn about people who fought to tell the stories of people who couldn't get their voices heard." Tony won't look at me. He is drawing on his paper, making random lines and shapes. Then Tony sighs. Long. Deep. "Reading this stuff over and over doesn't depress you?"

Essence says, "No."

I shake my head. "Not really. I mean, it's our country's history."

Tony keeps doodling.

I try to imagine how it must feel to sit here with two black girls and talk about how the people on this list reported about slavery, lynchings, the civil rights movement. I remember being in middle school and learning about all of this and coming home sad, frustrated. Blacks were always the victims, always having to fight for something. But Dad told me about scientists and inventors, and filled in the gaps that history books leave out. I know how I felt always being portrayed as the victim. I'm sure being seen as the perpetrator feels just as awful. "You should research them all," I say. "But especially Karl Fleming."

Essence flips through her notebook and reads from her notes. "He was a white journalist who covered some of the most known moments of the civil rights movement."

"It seems like he really cared about the stories he covered," I say. "He didn't just do it because it was a job. I found an article that talked about how he would vomit sometimes at the sight of dogs being loosed on protesters, how ashamed he was that he was from a place that had so much hate."

Essence shows Tony her scribbled notes as she reads them out loud. "He reported on the bombing of a church in Alabama, the desegregation of University of Mississippi, the assassination of Medgar Evers, and Freedom Summer of 1964."

"What is Freedom Summer?" Tony asks.

I shrug. "Something about voting, I think." I look through my notes and find the section about Freedom Summer. "Yeah, it was a campaign that started in June of '64 to register black voters in Mississippi."

Essence closes her notebook and leans back in her chair. "So wait, there's Freedom Summer and the Freedom Riders. What's the difference?" she asks.

I tell them the little I know. "The Freedom Riders were black and white activists who rode buses into the South together to protest and bring awareness to the rest of the nation about what was happening in the South."

Tony asks, "How do you know all this?"

"My parents had me and Nikki watch *Eyes on the Prize*, a documentary about the civil rights movement," I tell them. "And we didn't just watch it—my dad had us discuss it, you know, really understand what we were seeing."

Essence says, "God, Maya, your dad is like Martin Luther King, Cliff Huxtable, and Barack Obama all in one."

The three of us laugh.

Mrs. Armstrong walks to the front of the room. "Okay, everyone, let's hear back from each group."

We talk about what we've learned first, then why we think she wanted us to know.

Hands raise, and as Mrs. Armstrong calls on us, she writes key words on the board.

"Because it's Black History Month."

"To have us learn about local people as well as people outside of Oregon."

"To show us that words have power."

"Because you wanted us to know that no one can take our stories."

"Because you wanted to show us that both men and women, blacks and whites, worked for freedom."

When she is finished, the board is covered with our guesses of why she had us do this research.

Mrs. Armstrong doesn't even have to tell us the answer.

We're all right.

CHAPTER 50

Today, I have two posters. I get to school early. There's a janitor in the hallway near my locker and a teacher in her classroom next to the spot where I wanted to hang my posters. I walk around the school trying to find the perfect spot. The walls in junior hall are bare, except for two bulletin boards with student work on display. I hang my posters in the middle of the wall.

Karl Fleming, the journalist, and Jim Zwerg, a white freedom rider.

Above their photos and bios, I tape up the word *Allies*.

CHAPTER 51

We've all come together for an assembly. The one the school has every year to scare us out of drinking and driving. I am sitting next to Nikki, watching a slide-show of cars—and people—who have been damaged by drunk drivers. A mother who lost her son the night of his senior prom takes the microphone. There is a picture of her son that flashes on the screen, then a few slides of the car after the accident, which looks nothing like a car. Just mangled metal.

As she talks, she starts to cry a little. Two students behind me think this is funny. I turn around. It's Tasha sitting with her friends.

"*Shh*," I whisper.

"Oh, let's be quiet," Tasha says. "President Oreo can't hear."

The girl next to her whispers, "I can't stand fake people. She be tryin' to act like she down but really, she black on the outside, white on the inside."

They laugh.

"What did you say?" I ask.

"I didn't stutter. You ain't nothin' but an Oreo!" Tasha says.

"Ladies!" Mrs. Brown, one of the math teachers, whispers a shout and tells us to be quiet.

Tasha's friend won't let it go. She says to Tasha, "You should have called her a graham cracker!"

I have no idea what that's supposed to mean.

Tasha doesn't get the joke either. She asks, "Why would I call her that?"

" 'Cause she's brown and she's dating a cracker!"

They laugh.

The woman ends her speech, and Principal Green steps up to the mic and tells us that if any of us think we have a problem with alcohol or have a friend who has a problem to visit the counseling office. "You're dismissed," he says.

As Nikki and I walk out of the auditorium, my two new enemies walk past me. Tasha bumps into me on purpose. "Ignore her," Nikki says.

I stare her down.

"Maya, let's go."

Tony is standing a few steps away. Nikki points to him. "Let's go over there."

The eye roller sucks her teeth. "Yeah, go over there and be a sellout," she says.

Tasha looks Tony over. "What a rich white boy doin' so interested in putting on a black history celebration anyway?" she yells. "Why you trynna be in with us? What do you want?"

Tony stands mute.

I walk away, right past Tony. He follows me. "Maya. Wait up."

I just keep walking.

Nikki catches up with me. Tony is with her. "Why are you letting them get to you?" she asks.

"What happened?" Tony interjects before I can answer.

She tells him about the girls. About them calling me an Oreo, a sellout. "She thinks you and Maya are a couple or something, I think," Nikki explains.

Students pass us on their way to class. Nikki opens her locker and says, "Let it go, Maya. No need to get all worked up over a lie." She closes the locker and walks away, leaving Tony and me alone.

Tony walks across the hall to his locker; I stand next to him. We have journalism next. Might as well go together. Tony won't even look at me. "Sure you want to be seen standing next to me?" he asks.

"And what is that supposed to mean?"

He turns around, slams his locker, and walks away.

The tardy bell rings, and the last few students in the hall run to class. Tony and I walk together, but when we get to Mrs. Armstrong's class, he keeps walking. I go after him. "Tony."

He keeps walking.

"Tony!"

He turns left at the end of the hall, leaving me standing alone.

CHAPTER 52

When school is over I go straight home. By five o'clock it's already pitch-black outside. I am lying on my bed, listening to music and trying to sing my way out of this funky mood.

It's not working.

I have to tell Nikki what's going on. Essence, too. They are usually the people I go to when I have a problem. I keep wondering how I let it get to this, but I guess that doesn't matter.

I am waiting for Nikki to get home when the doorbell rings.

It's Tony. "Can we go somewhere to talk?" He jingles his keys. I leave a note for Mom and Dad and go with him.

I don't know where we're going. Tony drives toward Jantzen Beach and then heads north along the dark, narrow road following the length of the Columbia River. White sails sway in the wind against the black sky. If it were daylight, we could see Mount Hood peering over us, but tonight it's hidden, like it doesn't even exist. Portland's airport is on the right. The roar of planes taking off and landing fill the sky. Tony turns into an alcove and parks. He bends down and pulls the lever at the bottom of his seat and slides backward.

I take off my seat belt and pull my seat back. We sit and watch airplanes come and go.

Tony speaks first. "I'm sorry I walked away from you today. I'm just—why are we doing this?"

"What do you mean?"

"Why are we in a relationship if you don't want to be?"

"What do you have to be so high and mighty about? It's not like you're walking around telling everybody about me," I say.

"I've never lied about my relationship with you. If people ask, I tell the truth."

"Not to your father," I say.

Tony doesn't say anything.

"Does your father know about me?"

"That's different," Tony says.

"Really?"

"Yes, really." He stares out at the city.

"How is it different?"

"You don't understand my dad," he says. "Let's just leave it at that."

"Tony! All this talk about being true to yourself, all this talk about us not living in the fifties, and you can't tell your father you're dating a black girl?"

Tony refuses to answer me so we sit and watch planes. I am just about to give in and break the silence, but then Tony says, "I used to think my dad hated teaching, that he picked the wrong career. He always came home complaining about his day, telling me some story of a confrontation with a black student. Every day. And in every story there was this, this tone in his voice. Something like . . . something like, like disgust," Tony says. "The older I got and the more I listened, I realized it's not teaching he hates. He—look, my dad, he says horrible things about black people. And the way he talks about the students my mom advocates for? He says, he—he says horrible things." Tony stops talking, and I don't ask him anything, I just sit with him and we watch planes land and take off.

Then he turns to me. "He's not racist or anything, I mean, he just says, he just doesn't . . . Maya, I'm not ashamed of you. I'm ashamed of my dad. And afraid of what he'll say about you or to you."

Tony sits back up in his seat. "My mom knows about you. And so do my friends at St. Francis. I just haven't mentioned it to my dad. I don't think anything good would come of it, so what's the point?" Tony turns the car on.

I wonder what Portland looks like from the sky. Up there, rolling hills watch over the City of Roses, and the Fremont Bridge canopies over drivers coming and going from east to west. Up there it is just a normal winter day. In those clouds there are no traces of racial slurs being shouted in school halls, and the dust from the newly constructed buildings hasn't risen that far.

We leave Marine Drive and go home.

I ask, "So what are we going to do?"

Tony doesn't answer.

I get an upside-down feeling in my stomach. "You don't want to be with me anymore?"

"I do. I just, I need time to think."

As we ride home, I am thinking of Essence and Nikki right now. Thinking how maybe they are right. Maybe I should stick with what I know. What I know is Devin.

Tony pulls into his driveway.

"I guess Tasha has a point." I barely get the words out. "Blood is thicker than water."

Tony turns the engine off. "But you can't survive without either."

CHAPTER 53

We decide to go to the dance as girlfriends, instead of with dates. Kate is the one who suggested it. "My dad is more likely to let me go if he thinks I'm just going with friends," she said.

It's fine with me, since I don't have a date. I haven't talked to Tony for a week. I'm not sure if we're broken up or not. I guess he's still thinking. I don't even know if he's coming to the dance.

When we arrive at Richmond, I can't believe how different the gym looks. It has become a palace. The tables in the gym each have centerpieces with flowers floating in water. There is a photo backdrop with white pillars on each side and a fake staircase that looks like you can really walk up it. Music spills onto the dance floor, overflowing from the DJ's turntables. There are bodies all over bodies dancing and splashing in the sound waves.

Malachi, Ronnie, and Roberto are standing against the wall, looking too cool to dance, so we girls are on the dance floor together. Across the room, I see Devin dancing with Cynthia. I close my eyes and move to the beat.

We dance for three songs straight, but then a song comes on that none of us like, so Nikki and Essence persuade Ronnie and Malachi to get in line for pictures before they sweat out their hair.

Roberto, Kate, and I sit at a table with a few other girls who are giving their feet a break. Two girls I've never seen before come up to us. One has short red hair, the other, long gold curls. "Kate?"

They flock around Kate, who screams, "Oh, my God, what are you doing here?" She jumps up and hugs each of them.

The redhead says, "We came with them." She points over to Vince and Bags.

"Duh!" Kate says. "I forgot you went out with Vince."

Vince has a girlfriend? I feel sorry for her.

Kate introduces her St. Francis friends. The redhead seems nice. But Goldilocks barely acknowledges the rest of us. She sits down and starts gossiping with Kate. "I have to tell you the new news," she says. She dishes out all the scoop about St. Francis—which teachers are sleeping with each other, which students are using, who's had an abortion. She tells us how some sophomore at St. Francis got busted for drugs being in his locker. Apparently he'd been dealing at their school for the past two years.

I wonder why *that* didn't make the news.

"Hey, where's Tony?" Goldilocks asks. She stretches her neck out like an ostrich. The redhead joins her, standing on the tips of her toes like a ballerina.

"I see him! I see him!" Goldilocks yells. She is blushing and starts smiling and fixing her hair. "Oh, my God, Kate. Your brother is so hot."

Kate stands and waves him over. I turn and look behind me. Tony is walking toward us. Goldilocks is right. Tony looks good. And he's not even dressed up. He's in jeans and a T-shirt. Everything inside me trembles.

When Tony gets to the table, he only looks at me, as if no one else is sitting at the table, like he doesn't even know those other girls. "Will you come outside with me?" Tony asks.

Goldilocks looks completely annoyed that he didn't speak to her.

Kate smiles and gives me a reassuring look. I smile back at her.

Tony and I walk outside. I can hear the music

from inside vibrating the walls. One of my favorite songs. Tony stops just past the front door to the gym and turns to me. "I told my dad."

I don't say anything. Not because I don't want to, I just can't find the right words.

"Look, I know things are—"

I don't let Tony finish. I pull him close to me, and we kiss and hold each other. I know this doesn't mean things will be perfect, but I also know that this is what I want.

I hear the door open and close, then open and close again, and my lips don't pull away from his. The door opens once more and someone calls my name.

"Maya?"

I know that voice.

"Maya?"

It's Nikki.

CHAPTER 54

The next morning, I am up before the sun.

I stay in bed for a while, wishing I could fast forward through the explaining I'm going to have to do for the next couple of days. But I know I can't stay under these covers all day, so I get out of bed, shower, and go downstairs.

Dad is sitting at the dining room table drinking coffee and eating a toasted bagel. He starts his days early and always with caffeine. "How was it last night?" he asks. "Did Tony show up like I told him to?"

"What?" I sit next to Dad. "You talked to Tony?"

"I saw him sitting on his porch looking lovesick and pathetic. I've worked with young men for decades now. I know that look."

I can't help but smile at that part. I take half of his bagel and smother it with cream cheese.

"I asked him why he didn't take my beautiful daughter to the winter formal."

"How did you know about us?"

"I know everything," Dad says. He smiles and drinks from his mug.

"Dad—"

"I. Know. Everything," he repeats.

I laugh. And all I can say is, "Thank you."

"You don't ever have to hide things from us," Dad says. "And, you know, you can't control everything, Maya."

"Especially not my heart."

"Or anyone else's." Dad looks at me, and I look away because I don't want to cry. "If Nikki doesn't want to go to Spelman, you can't make her feel guilty about that. She has the right to change, Maya. So do you."

I lay my head on Dad's shoulder.

Dad hands me the other half of his bagel.

When Nikki comes into the kitchen, Dad gets up from the table and goes to the family room.

Nikki went out with Ronnie and the rest of the crew last night after the dance so we haven't talked at all yet.

She passes me without saying good morning and

goes straight into the kitchen. I can't see her, but I hear cereal pouring into a bowl, the opening of the fridge, a long pause, the pouring of milk, and the door of the fridge closing. A chair scrapes the kitchen floor, and I can tell that Nikki is sitting at the island.

I just want to get it over with so I start talking, not getting up from the dining room table, thinking maybe talking in separate rooms will ease the tension of a face-to-face conversation. "I'm sorry I lied to you, Nikki."

All I hear from her is the crunching of cereal.

Her spoon clanks against the bowl.

A full minute passes.

And then she says, "Why did you think you couldn't tell me?"

"I was going to. But—" I stop myself from making excuses. "I was ashamed. I was mad at myself for liking him. I mean, he's the guy who benefits from Essence having to move. How can I love him? And things at school have been so crazy. I just, I— Look, there's no good reason," I say.

I hear Nikki's chair rake the floor again, and then footsteps. She comes into the dining room. She just stares at me but at least we're in the same room.

"I'm sorry I lied, okay? But it took me a while to even admit it to myself. I was afraid—"

"Of what?" Nikki yells. "What could you possibly be afraid of?"

"Afraid that Tony would change me like Kate has changed you!"

With these words, I have officially ruined any chance of this being a kiss-and-make-up conversation. My words spill out of me by accident, like when someone knocks over a cup. They splash into the room, and I'm afraid that they will leave permanent stains on our relationship.

"What are you talking about? I haven't changed," Nikki says. "Just because I've made new friends doesn't mean I'm not the same person." Nikki goes back into the kitchen. "You really need to get over the fact my best friend is white."

Best? I've always been Nikki's best. And Essence has always been *our* best. I walk into the kitchen.

"How can you have a problem with me being Kate's friend when you're dating her brother?"

I get a glass out of the cabinet and hold it up to the refrigerator, pressing it against the water dispenser. "Look, Nikki, Tony is not changing me—not for the worse. He's not asking me to take him to Popeyes for *soul food*, and he's not surprised that I don't love hip-hop. He's not prancing me around—his new black friend—like I'm a trophy or something."

"Yeah, but he's hiding you. And that makes him better?"

I drink a sip of water. "I'm the one who didn't want anyone to know."

"You know, nobody cares if Maya Younger dates a white boy but you. Race doesn't matter anymore," Nikki says. "And for the record, I'm not mad that you're with Tony, a white boy. I'm upset because you lied about it."

"You can say all you want that race doesn't matter, but the reaction to those posters that hang on our school walls says it does, and Principal Green's overcompensation to make the white kids feel included says it does." I am yelling even though I am trying not to. I pause only to catch my breath. "And the difference between Tony and me is that we talk about these things. We address them. You and Kate want to function in this love-sees-no-color world, but if your friends don't see your color, then they don't see you. Because black is who you are, Nikki. And it matters."

I have a bad habit of always wanting the last word. I keep talking even though I know I should just apologize and walk away. "I like Kate, I do. I mean, she's actually grown on me. But really, it seems like every question she asks is about you being black, not about you being you."

Nikki stands up and washes her bowl. Her back is

to me, and we don't speak to each other for a while. The running water swallows the room's silence. "Sometimes I just want to exist, Maya. I can admit that Kate is annoying sometimes. But she's not racist. She's not asking us questions to be mean," Nikki says. "But the store clerks? Those people who watch me while I'm shopping in *their* stores—those are the people who get me. Okay, so maybe it matters. I get it. It's just exhausting to always have to respond to it." Nikki turns to me. "You know people call *you* the black one."

"Huh?"

"When people ask how do you tell the Younger twins apart, people say, 'Maya is the one who acts black. Nikki acts white,' " Nikki tells me. "And the first time I heard that, I confronted the person, made it a big deal. But then I just ignored them. Just kept being me. I'm not saying I'm right—it's just my way of dealing with things. I can't care too much. It, it—"

"Hurts."

"Yeah." Nikki sits next to me at the island. "I go to those stores because it's my way of standing up to it all, of telling them—and myself—that I belong, that I deserve this kind of stuff, too. Most times, it's not a problem, but I have definitely walked into one of the boutiques or restaurants on Jackson and felt people staring. Kate and I have gone places where the store clerk speaks only to her, helps only her. And I guess I could shop somewhere else, but I go because this is my neighborhood and I'm not going to hide. If they want to be here, then they're going to have to see me, learn how to interact with me."

There is silence again. Nikki's index finger traces invisible shapes on the island marble. I untwist and retwist my hair. Untwist and retwist.

"Am I a hypocrite?" I ask.

"You're a black girl who fell in love with a white boy."

"And a black girl who cares about race and class issues."

Nikki leans back in the chair. "You can be both."

CHAPTER 55

Mom tells me, "Some people will like you and some won't. What's more important is: Do you like yourself?"

I've been keeping that in mind today. I hear her saying it to me as I take Tony's hand and walk down senior hall.

There are stares and whispers, but we just keep walking. I don't let go of his hand.

CHAPTER 56

Team One is sitting in The Lounge complaining to Mrs. Armstrong about how we don't want to go to the diversity assembly.

"Why not?" Mrs. Armstrong puts her teacher voice on, like she doesn't already know why, like she is in support of the assembly. But I know that she and a few other teachers tried to get Principal Green to change his mind and have our annual black history celebration.

Tony, Charles, and I all look at one another trying to figure out who is going to answer her. Star won't make eye contact. She is giving her hand a tattoo with her blue marker. I am peeling an orange.

Charles speaks, telling all the reasons why we should go with tradition. And Tony adds our new idea about inviting Richmond alums as guest performers and speakers.

"All good reasons," Mrs. Armstrong says. "And I love your plan to bring alumni here." Mrs. Armstrong staples together sheets of paper, making the handouts for her next class. "So it seems you all want the same thing as Principal Green."

Star looks up. "No, that's the problem. Principal Green is on a completely different planet."

Staple, staple, staple. "Well, Charles just said that you all came up with an idea that will help people see the great things about Richmond. The legacy alumni have left behind, right?"

"Yes," I say. My orange has scented the entire room.

Mrs. Armstrong stacks her handouts on top of each other and walks to the whiteboard. "And you want to address the stereotypes people have about our school and prove them wrong, right?"

"Yes."

"Sounds like you and Principal Green want the same thing," she says. Her handwriting is in perfect print. "I'm sure if you propose that idea to him, he'd support it."

"We already did," I tell her.

Tony adds, "We wanted it to be in honor of Black History Month."

"I understand," Mrs. Armstrong says. "But think of it this way: When we're putting our newspaper together, what happens to really good articles that don't make the current issue being printed?"

"Depending on the timing, sometimes we publish them in the next one," Charles answers.

"Well?" Mrs. Armstrong asks.

"Well, what?"

"When is the next time Richmond will be having an event appropriate for what you want to do?"

"I don't know. The end-of-the-year block party, maybe?" I say.

"Find out," Mrs. Armstrong says.

Mrs. Armstrong walks through the aisles of the class and puts a handout on each table. I take half the stack out of her hands and help. The copies are on colored paper, so I know she spent her own money.

Mrs. Armstrong is on her second row when she asks, "Do you remember what we say makes a good title?"

"One that makes a reader want to read the article," I answer.

Mrs. Armstrong turns around and looks at me with a smile on her face. "Right. And does the writer get the last say on the title of their article?"

"No."

"Why?"

"Because sometimes an editor will change the title to reach a broader audience."

"Right again," Mrs. Armstrong says.

I hand her back the extra copies. She takes them out of my hand and then says to all of us, "These principles don't only apply to journalism."

CHAPTER 57

We found the student body presidents from the last decade. All it took was asking Dad, who asked a friend, who called another friend, and in two weeks we had everything we needed:

1. Mark Lewis has a master's in public health from Brown University. He runs a clinic in Philadelphia.

2. Martha Tucker went to Portland State University. She is a teacher at one of the middle schools that feed into Richmond.

3. Whitney Cunningham is a single mom of two boys. She took classes at Portland

Community College. She's very involved in her church.

4. Robert Graham owns a car repair shop down the street from Richmond.

5. Richard Martin is in the army.

6. Barbara Paterson attended seminary and is a chaplain at Good Samaritan Hospital in Northwest Portland.

7. Candy Stevenson went to Juilliard and dances in Broadway musicals.

8. Rose Franklin is a real estate agent.

9. Harold Milner graduated from Western Seminary and is the pastor of a church in downtown Portland.

10. Destiny Villa, who graduated last year, got a full-tuition scholarship to University of Oregon.

We have a lot to be proud of. And that's just ten people.

CHAPTER 58

It is the last day of February. The sun is shining but giving no heat. Sunshine can be deceiving. Today is Richmond's diversity celebration. The program starts off with dances from Japan, India, and Hawaii. Then Principal Green introduces our guest diversity speaker, Vicki Franklin. We welcome her to the stage with half-sincere applause.

She starts off by saying, "We have more similarities than we do differences." And then she does this dramatic pause like she's just said something profound. From there, it just goes downhill. Most of the students are texting or playing games on their cell phones. A few are asleep.

After the assembly, the dismissal bell rings, but I can't go home. Principal Green has called a special student council meeting after school. Vicki wants to meet the student leaders. When I walk into the room, she is sitting at the head of the table, all smiles.

Principal Green waits until all of us are seated and then starts the meeting. He turns to our guest. "Vicki, the floor is yours."

"First off, let me say that I've had such a great time today. Before I leave, I wanted to talk with a core group of you because I've been made aware of what's been happening here." Vicki taps Principal Green on his shoulder. And he jumps up, realizing he missed his cue.

Principal Green stands and walks over to his closet. He takes out a thin cardboard box. His plump hands grab a pair of scissors and he cuts the clear tape. The box cracks open. He pulls out an assortment of posters.

Vicki takes one and holds it up. "We'd like each of you to take a few posters and hang them up around the school. As student leaders, it's important that you are seen taking a stand for unity in the school."

Principal Green chimes in. "We also think the school could use a little inspiration. Just a little inspiration. So we want to have positive messages all around the building to motivate you all and to keep you focused on graduating."

Like a poster is going to get us to graduate.

Principal Green and Vicki pass out the posters. The one on top has the symbol for peace in the middle of the page, with the word PEACE written in several languages within the sign.

Tasha has a flyer that shows a welcome mat. The words on the mat read DIVERSITY WELCOMED HERE.

I see Charles looking through the posters and scrunching his face into a frown when he sees one that says THE ONLY THING IN YOUR WAY IS YOU.

Tell that to Essence.

Tony gets a poster that has a black male offering a Latina student a joint. The girl in the poster is walking away from him toward a group of students waiting for her. The caption reads IT'S OKAY TO WALK AWAY.

Principal Green gives me a poster that has two white students, one male, the other female. They are in their graduation gowns and tossing their caps in the air. They have big smiles on their faces and the caption reads SUCCESS AWAITS YOU.

I grab the drug poster out of Tony's hand and point to the black and Latina faces and ask, "How come *their* faces are on the poster about drugs and not on *this* one?" I hold the two posters next to each other.

Inspirational messages?

"Well, we didn't make the posters, Maya," Principal Green says.

"You bought them, though," I say.

Vicki clears her throat and says in a calm therapist voice, "It sounds like you're having some negative feelings about this. Would you like to share what emotion you're feeling right now?"

I imagine her working with a client and asking him to point to some stupid chart that has all kinds of facial expressions that range from the best kind of happiness to the worst type of sad. "I'm fine," I say.

"Does anyone else have something they need to share?" Vicki asks.

Cynthia looks at Tasha, then says, "Well, I mean—it's obvious why Maya doesn't want to use these posters. She's the one keeping the poster war going."

Star yells, "Well, who's the one defacing them and writing inappropriate messages? You?"

For the first time, I think maybe it is Cynthia. And then I look at Vince and Bags, and I know they must have something to do with it, too. They are too quiet. They are never quiet.

Cynthia says, "It's got to be her. All the posters that keep being hung on the walls are about people we've studied in Mrs. Armstrong's class," She looks at me like she's just won some kind of battle.

Principal Green looks at me, leans forward in his chair.

"It's me," Charles says. "I'm the one who's been hanging the posters."

Tony rubs the back of his neck. "I've hung some, too," he says.

And Star says, "I think they are trying to take the blame for me, Principal Green."

I am surprised when Joey and Rachel confess that they are the ones who have been putting up the posters.

Tasha blurts out, "Oh, God, what is this, some kind of Disney special? Maya did it. The rest of them are just—"

"Principal Green," I say. "You can suspend me. That's fine. Cynthia is right. I'm the person who's been putting up the posters. I haven't written anything derogatory, but I have been the one putting up some of the black history posters."

Principal Green looks at me. "I must say, I am very disappointed in you." He leans back in his chair, and I wait to hear what my consequence will be.

CHAPTER 59

Principal Green wants to speak to all of us individually. He talks to Joey first, then Rachel. Tony is next, and then he calls on Charles, then Star. I go in last.

"I can't have the student body president breaking the rules," he says.

"I know. But I can't be the student body president and not fight for the students."

Principal Green sighs. "Fight for the students? Just what exactly are you fighting for?"

"For our right to learn our history—and by *our* I don't mean black. I mean everyone's history. You want us to chant about being each other's keeper, but when we tried to hold each other accountable, you didn't let us. That assembly is something that gave us pride, and you took it away from us. You came here and started making all these changes without letting us be a part of it. And maybe I didn't go about this the right way, but at least you know why I did it." I am either going to get in a lot of trouble with Mom and Dad for talking to an adult this way or they will be proud.

Principal Green sits quietly. He turns in his office chair a few times, slow, like moving back and forth is helping him think.

I say, "And Mrs. Armstrong had nothing to do with this. She didn't tell us to do it or anything. All she did was teach us."

He is still quiet, still turning. Then he says, "I can't prove who's been responding to your posters, but since you have confessed to being the one who started this, I have to suspend you. Two days."

I must admit, I am relieved. I thought he might say that I can't be student body president anymore or that I can't participate in senior activities. I've made it through elementary, middle, and three and half years of high school without being suspended until now. Nikki is never going to let this go.

"I need to call your parents," he says.

"Okay."

Principal Green stands, and I take this as my cue that our talk is over. I get up, too, but just before I walk out, I turn to him and say, "I don't know if you want my idea or not, but I think I know what we can do for the senior block party." I don't even give him a chance to say this isn't the time. I just keep talking. "Remember when we talked about bringing alumni to the school to give motivational speeches?"

"Of course, of course."

"Remember how you wanted us to find alumni who weren't athletes?"

"Yes. Yes, I do."

"Well, we found some," I tell him. I go into my backpack and take out my folder.

I have nothing to lose. It's time for the pitch.

SPRING

CHAPTER 60

March.

Rain lingers, promising flowers on the other side of the storm. Clocks move forward and daylight visits us longer, stays through evening, keeping us company. The morning light whispers to me, calling me out of bed.

I am awake, alive.

CHAPTER 61

I'm on my second day of suspension, but it feels like I've missed a whole week of school already. I get the recap from Nikki and Essence, and then at night Tony calls and he fills me in on anything they left out.

Tonight we are standing at our windows talking to each other. Tony is walking around his room putting away clothes from a laundry basket. He has me on speaker phone, so sometimes when he talks, his voice sounds far away or he disappears and I can't see him.

"Will you be still?"

"I'm almost done," he says. "So anyway, this is what Principal Green agreed to. He liked our idea and said that we can invite alumni to the block party if we also invite local businesses," Tony tells me. "Charles and Star think it's a good idea."

I turn my light off, turn on a lamp, and lean against my window.

"We'll ask some of the restaurants to donate food, and we'll set up booths so that businesses can hand out flyers, freebies, you know. Promote their store."

"And what did Team Two think?"

"They like the idea, too."

We actually agree on something. "Good, that's good."

Tony hangs up a shirt in his closet. "So what were you doing before I called?"

"Getting your birthday gift together," I say. His birthday is in two days.

"What did you get me?"

"Like I'm really going to tell you."

"Well, you can give me a hint."

"I can't give you a hint. It will make it too obvious."

"P*leeease*." Tony has walked out of my sight.

"Come back to the window. I want to see you."

Tony reappears. "P*leeease*."

"Okay, here's a hint," I tell him, and then I start singing a slow, soft melody from one of the songs I just burned on a CD for him. At first my voice comes out like a whisper and my insides are shivering because I don't know what he will think of my voice. But then I close my eyes and sing as if Tony isn't listening, like I do in the shower or when I'm in my room all by myself and no one's home.

As I sing the last lyric, I open my eyes. Tony has the phone off speaker and is holding it up to his ear. He's at the window.

I keep singing, even though I'm at the end of the song.

CHAPTER 62

This morning Mom got a phone call from Ms. Thelma's son. He told her that Ms. Thelma passed away in her sleep last night. I haven't seen the old woman in years, but, still, my eyes burn and all I can think of is her house that is now a coffee shop. I want to go back there, to what was. I want to sit with her and listen to her remake endings to stories she could no longer remember.

I walk around the corner to Jackson Avenue and slowly make my way down the long street. I get to Daily Blend, but I don't go in. Not right away. I wait for the crowd to thin out, wait till the tables are free and the line is short. When I step into the coffee shop, I go to the counter and order tea.

"What size would you like?"

"Oh, uh, small," I say. I pay for the tea and wait.

I had forgotten about my tears until the girl taking my order gives me a sympathetic smile and says, "This pollen is crazy, isn't it? My eyes were all messed up yesterday, too. Allergy season is upon us."

I smile, take the mug, and sit down next to the window at the front of the house. I close my eyes, and I can almost hear Ms. Thelma, feel her. I remember her hugs. How they were just as comforting as chicken noodle soup. I remember the way she made tea. Black, with a teaspoon of honey and two squirts of lemon. I sip. Everything feels and looks so new. There are black-and-white photographs lining the wall. I stand up and walk over to take a closer look.

There is an elderly man sitting at a table next to the wall. I smile.

He nods hello.

I stand at the wall looking at the photos. The pictures are of Portland. The first one I notice is a picture of a street sign that says UNION AVENUE.

"That's what it was called 'fore they named it Martin Luther King Jr. Boulevard," the man says. He chuckles and takes a sip from his mug. "We were all up in arms 'bout them givin' such a sleazy street to an honorable man." The man tells me about all the many stages MLK has seen—how the street used to be a haven for car dealerships in the forties and then a strip for prostitutes in the eighties.

He stands up slowly and joins me at the wall. "And this photo right here is what I like to call Portland's Little Harlem." He points to a picture. "This right here is Louis Armstrong with the owners of Dude Ranch; uh, this one is, uh, Pat Patterson . . . and *his* name is Sherman Pickett." He turns away from the gallery and says, "I'm Mr. Washington, by the way."

"Maya."

"You're one of the Younger twins, yes?"

"Yes."

"Your dad is doing good things, very good."

"Thank you."

We shake, and his hands feel weak and cold. Mr. Washington walks over to his table and pulls out a chair, motioning for me to join him. I sit down. "Now," he says. "Where was I? Oh, yes, Dude Ranch." He takes a sip of his steaming coffee and says, "Dude Ranch was Portland's premier jazz club. It brought in some of the best. Why, even Thelonious Monk played there."

I don't know who Thelonious Monk is, but he must be someone important. I look back over at the photo. "Where is this?" I ask.

"That there is North Broadway," he says. "You know, not too far from Williams Avenue."

"Do you mind if I write this down?" I ask.

"Why, no. Not at all."

I go into my bag, get my pen and notepad.

Mr. Washington takes another sip of his coffee. "Williams Ave was the heartbeat of the black community back in the forties. All kinds of performances would happen in the clubs—live jazz, tap dancers, talent shows. Yes, indeed. That's why I call it Portland's Harlem," Mr. Washington says. "And the food. My Lord, the food. There were restaurants that stayed open all night serving that good ole bar-b-que." Mr. Washington looks at my necklace. He leans forward and squints a little to get a good look, then says, "But I reckon you already know most of this stuff since you're wearing something like that around your neck."

I look down at my necklace. What is he talking about? I lift it up a little. "This?"

Mr. Washington smiles. "That symbol is no ordinary bird. You know that, right?"

"No, I—it's just a necklace."

"No, no. It's not just a necklace. That there is the Adinkra symbol from Ghana. Sankofa."

"Sankofa?"

"It means 'return and get it.' It's a symbol to

remind us of the importance of remembering our past," Mr. Washington says. "And not just remembering, but taking lessons from the past and bringing it into the present in order to make progress."

I hold the necklace in my hand. I can't believe that all this time I'd been carrying something so meaningful with me every day. I say the word in my head a few times. San-ko-fa. Sankofa, sankofa. I write it down.

Mr. Washington stands and goes back to the wall. "Maya, right?" he asks.

"Yes."

"Let's go back and get it." He points to another photograph. An area shot of the Albina neighborhood. Mr. Washington points to where Emanuel Hospital is. "When Emanuel first expanded, those of us living in the area protested it. Got tired of them moving us out." He tells me that in the seventies hundreds of homes were destroyed so that the hospital could expand. "An urban renewal project, they called it. Displaced a lot of families. Most of us black, you know." Mr. Washington sits back down at the table.

I sit across from him and sip my tea, which is cold now.

"And it wasn't the first time the city tried to break us up. In the fifties it was them building that Memorial

Coliseum and in the sixties, I-5. Every decade, it's something. Been that way since the Vanport flood. You know about the flood, yes?"

"I know there was a flood that destroyed an area where a lot of black people lived."

"That's all that's left of the story, huh?" Mr. Washington leans in to the table. "A lot of blacks migrated to Portland during World War II because there were a lot of jobs in the shipyards. Vanport was a temporary settlement for war workers and their families," he says. "In 1948 the Columbia River flooded Vanport. I believe they say seventeen thousand people were left homeless—most of us black." Mr. Washington shakes his head at the memory. "Before the flood actually happened, Portland's Housing Authority told the people everything would be fine, that they'd be warned if necessary. But nothing was fine. That levee that the government built, it broke, and a ten-foot wall of water washed the city away. Now, where were blacks supposed to go after that? Why, in 1940 there was roughly, oh, about eighteen hundred blacks in Oregon. I'm told by '48 there was close to fifteen thousand. Portland didn't know what to do with us."

I can't believe I've never heard any of this. Not even from Dad.

Mr. Washington looks out the window, then back at me. "And after the war, we couldn't get no work, couldn't buy no homes. We were banned from whole neighborhoods." He leans back in his chair. The history-book man takes one last sip of his coffee, turning the cup all the way up to get the last drop. He laughs to himself at a joke only he knows and says, "But then Berry came on the scene. You know about Bill Berry, don't you?"

I try to think fast. I know the name, I know the name. Just when it comes to me, Mr. Washington says, "He was the president of the Urban League. They called him here from New York, thinking he'd come and help them solve their Negro problem. Wanted him to convince us to leave, get the blacks who had come to work in the shipyards to go back to wherever we were from. But Berry had another plan."

Mr. Washington takes out a handkerchief to wipe his nose. "He used to say to them white folks, 'You can't have it both ways. Can't call us lazy but on the other hand won't let us work.' " He closes his eyes and pauses, and I wonder if he can hear these words as he tells them to me. "He'd say, 'If you arrange it so they don't have jobs, then you are setting up a system where you will have to support them.' That's what he'd tell 'em. He'd say, 'They either gonna steal or beg, so your options are to give them an opportunity to work and earn their rightful wage or support them.' "

Mr. Washington laughs loud and long. "And you

know, some people heard him. They got it, and they started hiring us and housing us, but many of them paid for it—whites who treated black folk friendly weren't too popular. Not everyone wanted blacks to thrive here."

"I never knew this kind of thing existed in Portland," I say.

"Fear exists everywhere," he tells me. "There are always man-made borders—seen and unseen—to keep certain folk in or out. Like the Laurelhurst pillars."

"The stone pillars by the park?"

"They built that section of the city to be homes for the high class. Restrictions were put on that side of town."

"What do you mean?"

"The sale of alcohol was prohibited, there couldn't be any apartments, and no homes were to be sold to the Chinese or Japanese or black folk." Mr. Washington's voice gets real serious, real stern. "Now I've never known there to be a restriction on the selling of alcohol where the black folk live. What you think that means?"

Mr. Washington leans back in his chair. "But we had help. You know, every struggle has allies. Ah, let's see, Russell, uh, Russell Payton, a white civil rights leader, and then there was Hatfield—the governor in, oh, I think it was '59 and well into the sixties. Yes, yes, we have had and still have allies," he says.

The coffee shop is getting crowded again, and people are walking around looking for tables to sit at. "I guess we should be neighborly and let someone else have a turn," Mr. Washington says. He crumples his napkin and backs away from the table.

"Thank you for talking to me," I say.

We stand, push our chairs in, and take our mugs to the rack for dirty dishes. "You're welcome," he says. "You look just like your mother," he tells me. "Tell Yvette and Thomas that I said hello, okay?"

As we walk to the door, Mr. Washington says, "It's important to know the story. Your story. Keep asking questions. Make folk tell you."

"I will."

We walk out of the door, onto Jackson Avenue, and go opposite ways. I turn quickly, and call out to him. "Mr. Washington, how do you feel about this?" I point out at the block, the traffic, the shops and galleries.

"Most of these folk are just good people trying to make a livin', I suppose. If having them here means more stop signs and handicapped-accessible sidewalks, then so be it. Those of us black folk who do own our homes, who aren't itching to sell, have seen the value of our property rise. It's not all bad. Nothing ever is," Mr. Washington says. "Now, just looking at it from a business standpoint—they need us and we need them. They need us to come in to their stores, and we need them to come out into the community and get involved."

Cars drive by looking for spaces to park. A long line of cyclists ride, single file, down the bike lane.

"Thanks again for talking with me," I say.

"Anytime. Anytime. When you want some more, just come on by. I get my cup of joe once a day," he tells me. "You have a good day now, you hear?" Mr. Washington walks away.

I go back into the coffee shop, ask to speak to the owner. She wipes her hands on her apron and shakes my hand. "Hi, I'm Mandy. How can I help you?"

"I'm Maya. I'm here representing Richmond High School," I tell her. "I'd like to invite you to participate in our block party. Do you have a moment to talk?"

CHAPTER 63

Essence is over, and we are wasting a Sunday by eating every kind of junk food in the house and watching a marathon of the most depressing made-for-TV movies ever. A commercial comes on for the beauty school that's downtown.

"Turn that up!" Essence sits up on the bed, grabs a pen from my nightstand, and writes the number down on one of the pages of her hair magazine. "I've been meaning to look them up. I'm thinking about applying there."

"Why?" I ask. Like I don't know the answer.

"Maya, I'm not going to Spelman, okay? It's not going to work."

"You don't know that it's not going to work out," I say.

"I don't have money for a school like that. Plus, I want to do hair. Doesn't it make sense to go to a school that's going to help me do what I want to do?"

"Is that all you want to do? Style hair?" I don't mean to belittle her.

"What are you trying to say?" Essence closes her magazine and tosses it across the bed.

I think about Mr. Washington and everything he told me, think about how he called Williams Avenue Portland's Harlem, and I wonder if it could ever be that again. "If you want to do hair for a living, that's fine. But at least take business classes so you own your own shop and don't just work in one."

"Maybe I want to 'just do hair'!" Essence shouts.

"But think of what you could do. You could own the hair salon. Make it a spa, make it upscale. I mean, maybe one day you could open your own place over here and instead of all these white people taking over and buying up everything, another black business could start. That's all I'm saying, you know?"

Essence starts gathering her stuff. "I'm not like you, Maya, with all your big dreams about changing the world. I'm simple. I just want to be regular. I just want a decent job, to get married, have a few kids, enjoy life. I can do that without Spelman." She starts to walk out but then turns and adds, "I've wanted a lot of things. I wanted to be the first person in my family to not just go to college, but graduate and then go on and get my master's, and even a PhD." Essence gets lost in her memories and smiles to herself. "Imagine me, a black girl from Northeast Portland getting a PhD." She stops smiling and now her voice is sad, almost angry. "You are right, I had lots of goals. Remember how bad I wanted my mom to be sober? I wanted that real bad. But I learned that just 'cause you want something don't mean it's going to happen."

CHAPTER 64

The thing about Essence is that yesterday is yesterday. She doesn't hold grudges, and she knows that no matter if we disagree, we love each other and we'll always have each other's back. So that's why I'm not surprised when she whispers to me, "Don't let them trifling girls get to you," as we walk down the hallway.

Something bad is about to happen.

It's in Tasha's eyes, a look that says she wants trouble, is looking for it. She is standing with Cynthia at the end of the hall. Essence, Nikki, and I are walking toward them, and when we get to my locker, which is across from Tasha's, I hear her say, really loud, loud enough for everyone in the noisy hallway to hear, "There go the sellout girls."

Essence stands in front of me. "What did you say?"

Tasha leans back against her locker. She looks me up and down and mumbles something under her breath.

"What did you say?" I ask.

Essence says, "Don't worry about her. She's just mad because she doesn't have what you have. You know, a boyfriend who loves her, real friends who care." Essence rolls her eyes and turns around to open her locker.

Now Tasha is standing behind her, so close Essence barely has room to turn around. "I might not have what Maya has, but I have more than you. A mother who cares about me."

It happens quicker than a blink, faster than the second hand on a clock. Essence and Tasha are tangled in a knot hitting each other and rolling on the floor fighting. It takes both of our security guards and a teacher to break them up.

Principal Green comes out into the hallway. "You all just stood here and watched? None of you thought to get an adult? Come on, Richmond, we're better than this. Let's be better than this," he says. "We are our brother's keeper."

I know Principal Green means well, but it's going to take more than a chant to fix this.

CHAPTER 65

In journalism we review what's in the news, and then Mrs. Armstrong releases us to work on our individual articles for the school paper. A few students go to the back of the room to begin typing their stories for our next issue. I am looking through my notes on the interview I did of Mr. Corbett—the teacher who's been at Richmond the longest. Just when I get up to head to the computer space, the door swings open.

"Essence? Essence, you in here?" It's Ms. Jackson. And she is completely wasted. Her twig legs barely keep her standing.

And her record keeps spinning.

"Where's my baby? Where's my daughter?" Ms. Jackson walks through the rows of desks looking for Essence, who is sitting at a computer at the back of the room. "I'm here for the parent meeting! Where the meeting at? I'm here!" she shouts. She is holding the letter that the school sent home with Essence when they suspended her for the fight.

Mrs. Armstrong stands and approaches Ms. Jackson. "Hi, hello, our, uh, our meeting is at 3:00, and it's only 1:30. Do you mind coming back?" Mrs. Armstrong says.

Students are laughing, and some are in such shock they can't even muster a giggle. Essence doesn't move. She just sits at the computer like that isn't her drunk mother who just showed up for a parent meeting an hour and a half early.

Mrs. Armstrong gently touches Ms. Jackson's arm. "Come with me," she says.

"I ain't goin' nowhere with you! I done came all the way over here, and you just gonna send me home. What I look like to you? Look like I got all the time in the world, do I? Well, I don't. I ain't got time to be sittin' round here waitin' on you. Just tell me what you got to tell me!"

Mrs. Armstrong tries to remove her again. "Ms. Jackson, please. Let me walk you to the main office. You can wait there."

"I told you I ain't goin' nowhere!" Ms. Jackson makes her way past Mrs. Armstrong and sees me. "You seen Essence?"

"Ms. Darlene, the meeting is after school. Why don't you let me take you outside," I say. From the corner of my eye, I see Mrs. Armstrong on the phone. It doesn't take long before security is in the classroom.

Essence gets up and stuffs her notebook in her bag.

"There you are, baby, why you ain't said nothin'? I been lookin' for you." She reaches out for Essence, but Essence moves away from her and leaves the classroom.

Ms. Jackson morphs from the sweet, funny drunk to an outraged woman. She is cursing and yelling now, and calling Essence all kinds of names no mother should ever call her child.

"Ms. Jackson, please come with me," William, one of our security guards, says. He takes her out.

Mrs. Armstrong closes the door.

There are no discreet giggles, just full-blown hysterical laughter coming from everyone except me, Tony, and Charles. Mrs. Armstrong hushes the room, tells everyone to stop laughing and get back to work. Before I can even ask to be excused, Mrs. Armstrong looks at me and says, "Go check on her."

I check every crevice of Richmond, but I can't find Essence.

I call her cell phone, but she doesn't answer. I try again. No answer. I hang up.

There's only one more place I can think of to

look. I leave school and walk home, and as soon as I turn the corner onto my block, I see Essence sitting on the porch swing of her old house. There are no cars in the driveway, which means both of Tony's parents are gone, which is good. I'm sure they'd freak out if they saw some random girl swinging on their porch.

I walk up the steps and sit next to Essence. We swing and sway and rock to Essence's blues.

Back and forth.

Back and forth.

Down the block, I see Mom driving. She pulls into our driveway and when she gets out, she sees us sitting on the porch. I take Essence by the hand, and we walk across the street. I tell Mom what happened.

"Get in," she says. Mom drives to Essence's house and before we get out of the car, she turns to Essence and says, "When we go inside, I don't want you to say a word. Not one word. Just go to your room and start packing."

CHAPTER 66

"Melvin, is that you?" Ms. Jackson yells from her bedroom.

"No, Darlene, it's me," Mom says.

"Who is 'me'?" Ms. Jackson comes out of her room. When she sees Mom, she walks over to her and stands as close as she can get. Mom doesn't back up. "What you want?" Ms. Jackson says.

Essence obeys Mom's orders and goes to her room to pack. I go with her.

We leave the door open and listen. Mom says, "You broke our agreement."

Ms. Jackson starts to pout like a child. "Please don't do this. One more chance. One more chance," she says.

"No, Darlene. No more chances. Essence is moving in with me."

Essence and I look at each other. She packs faster.

"Don't do this to me. Come on, I just been havin' a hard time," Ms. Jackson says.

"Darlene, are you going to your meetings?"

"No."

"Are you using again?" Mom asks.

Ms. Jackson doesn't answer.

"There are no more chances. She's coming with me. That was the agreement. You promised me and Thomas that you'd stay clean, get treatment, attend your support group—do whatever it takes to keep it together—and you're not doing anything." Mom is a quiet storm. But as strong as she is, I can hear the tears at the back of her throat trying to stay at bay. "Darlene, I've known you over half of my life. I care about you and Essence—"

"I know, I know. You ain't been nothin' but good to me," Ms. Jackson says. "I'm gonna get myself together. I am," she says.

Essence zips her suitcase, I zip the duffel bag, and we come out into the living room. When Ms. Jackson sees us, she reaches out for Essence, who pulls away. "Baby, I'm gonna get it together. I promise. I'll do it for real this time," she swears. "You gonna stay with them for just a little while, till I get back on my feet."

Essence goes outside to the car. I stand at the door, waiting for Mom.

"I love my daughter. I do. I tell you the truth, I love my baby girl and I'm gonna do right. I am."

Mom says good-bye to Ms. Jackson, and we leave her standing at the door, singing the same lyrics she's been serenading Essence with her whole life. "I'm gonna get better. You'll see, you'll see."

CHAPTER 67

My family hasn't had breakfast together for weeks. Mom has been trying to establish Saturday breakfast since January—as part of her New Year's resolution to get us to spend more time with one another. It's the end of March and so far we've only had Saturday breakfast together twice.

Essence thinks it's funny that we even try to have a meal together.

Just when we sit down at the dining room table, the doorbell rings. "I'll get it," I say. I get up from the table, walk to the door, and look through the peephole. "Dad, it's Principal Green."

Dad jumps up from the table. "Oh, no! I forgot about our breakfast meeting at Village Inn."

Mom sets down her coffee. "You mean you forgot not to schedule anything on Saturday mornings."

"This is important."

"Two hours. Your family just wants two hours," Mom says.

"Honey, I'm sorry." Dad kisses Mom on her forehead.

I open the door. Principal Green comes in, and I am hoping no one sees the principal coming to my house.

Principal Green is casual today. Jeans and a polo shirt.

"Jimmy," Dad says. "Be with you in a moment."

"My, it sure smells good in here," Principal Green says. "Looks like we don't need to get our own breakfast. Looks like we don't need to get our own breakfast at all." He takes in an exaggerated whiff of Mom's cooking.

"Would you like to stay here and meet?" Mom asks, dry and flat.

"Do you mind? Do you?" Principal Green is in the dining room faster than my mom can even think about it.

"I'll fix you a plate," Mom says. She gives Dad her look of death but gets up and fixes Principal Green a plate of pancakes with strawberries on top. "My only rule is no business until we're finished with breakfast," Mom says.

Principal Green smiles. "Deal. Oh, yes, you've got a deal."

We eat breakfast, and most of the conversation is about the weather. I have kitchen duty this week, so when we're finished eating, I clean the table and load the dishwasher. Nikki and Essence go upstairs. I've set freshly brewed cups of coffee on the table for Dad and Principal Green. They've turned the dining room into a boardroom, and papers are spread out all over the table.

"Thomas, brotha, Richmond can't thank you enough. A full-tuition scholarship? We sure are going to make some family's load a lot lighter. Yes, indeed. Someone's load is going to be a lot lighter."

A scholarship for a Richmond student? I immediately think about all the friends I have who need this.

"Don't thank me. Thank my funders. And Susan Jacobs," Dad says.

Susan Jacobs? That's Tony's mom.

"Without them, I couldn't allocate anything. It's been great partnering with her organization."

Principal Green slurps his coffee. "Now, what are the restrictions of the award? And what should be our guidelines?"

I wipe down the countertops and hand wash the pans and dishes that are too big for the dishwasher. I usually clean with music blasting. But today I want to hear every word that's being said.

Dad says, "The scholarship can be used on anything school related. Tuition, books, room and board, computer, living expenses. Whatever."

Principal Green says, "Now, as far as GPA, what did you have in mind?"

Dad comes into the kitchen to get milk for his coffee. His voice rises above the running water. "I'd like to see this go to a student who might not have the best grades but has contributed to the community through leadership and service and has potential to excel in college if given the opportunity."

Yes! Essence definitely fits in that category, and of course Charles does, too. Every summer we volunteer at Dad's center working as support for the summer camp counselors who teach the elementary kids.

Principal Green says, "We've got to be careful with that, Thomas. We can't let it look like Richmond is rewarding mediocrity."

"There's nothing mediocre about leadership and service," Dad says. He continues with his list, "I also think we should require that applying students be students who've attended Richmond for at least two years."

"There's no way we can put a stipulation like that

on this scholarship. We can't exclude new students from applying."

"We can't let a student that's been at Richmond for one year walk away with the Leadership Scholarship either."

"And why not?"

I am done cleaning the kitchen, but I want to hear all their conversation. I clean the microwave. It's not too dirty, but it could use a good wipe down.

Principal Green lowers his voice like he's releasing top-secret information. "Look, Thomas. As the kids say, let me keep it real with you." He chuckles, as if he's proud of using slang. "As you know, enrollment at Richmond is at an all-time low. And it just doesn't make sense. There are too many students living in Richmond's district," he says. He slurps his coffee between sentences. "Northeast Portland is not a black community anymore."

His voice gets even lower; I strain to hear him. "I'd like us to make sure we are giving the scholarship to recipients that show the wide range of students we have at Richmond. You know, to show how diverse we are," Principal Green says. "You see, we need to change the face of Richmond. We've got to. We have to show our, uh, new parents that this school isn't just an urban school, if you know what I mean. They need to see their faces up there getting awards and being involved in assemblies and programs, or they'll send their kids elsewhere."

Dad clears his throat. "We're keeping it real, right?" he says sarcastically.

"Keeping it real, yes," Principal Green says.

"Well, let's stop beating around the bush. Are you asking me to preselect a recipient and to make sure that the recipient is not African American?"

Principal Green's voice gets lower and lower. "I'm asking you to make sure there is clear representation of Richmond's *diverse* student body."

Dad gets his professional voice on. "A panel of judges determines the winner. Neither you nor I can be on the panel. We shouldn't even touch an application. And the ethnicity of the applicant will not be relevant."

Dad stands and walks Principal Green to the door.

I put the dustpan and broom away and walk out into the living room.

Principal Green shakes Dad's hand. "Thank your wife for me for the delicious breakfast. I'll be in touch."

As soon as the door closes I think of all the questions I have about what I just overheard.

Dad knows me well. Before I can even get the words out of my mouth he says, "Not now, Maya."

"But Dad, can I just say one thing—just one?"

"Not now, Maya," he says.

"I just have one question."

"One," Dad says.

"When are applications going to be ready?"

"You can't apply. It wouldn't look right if one of my daughters—"

"I'm not asking for me."

"I'll have everything ready by Wednesday."

"Okay," I say.

"Is that all?"

"Yeah, you said I could only say one thing."

"It's a miracle," Dad says. And he laughs and puts his heavy hand on my shoulder. "Sorry I ruined breakfast," he says.

"You didn't ruin anything," I tell him. "You just saved Essence's dream."

CHAPTER 68

Essence and I are in the office to pick up applications for the scholarship. I'm getting two. One for Charles, one for Ronnie. Essence is getting hers and Malachi's.

"They're due in two weeks," Ms. Joan, the secretary, says. "Just come back and put it in that box, and then you'll be contacted about an interview."

"An interview?" I ask.

"Each finalist will sit down with the judging committee for a brief interview. You two should have nothing to worry about," she says. "There are only four questions."

Just then, Principal Green's door opens and Cynthia is walking out of his office. She has an application in her hand.

I figured he'd encourage her to apply, but I wonder what they were talking about behind his closed door. "Thanks, Ms. Joan," I say. I look at Principal Green, make sure he sees that I see him. He looks away.

Once we leave the office, Essence and I go our separate ways. I'm going to Mrs. Armstrong's class. Essence is going to do hair. When I get to class, I get right to work on my article for the school newspaper. I've been assigned the story on our block party and eighth-grade recruitment day.

Mrs. Armstrong says a good journalist always has her eyes open, always has an ear listening for news. So when I hear Cynthia say to Tasha, "These interview questions are hard," my antenna goes up and I pick up every whisper between the two of them. "He says I should practice my answers," Cynthia says. And then Mrs. Armstrong walks by so she stops talking. I see her slide a sheet of paper into her notebook, and I decide that I will do whatever I have to do to get those questions.

Attempt One. I get up and purposely walk into Cynthia's desk. I make sure I act real clumsy and knock her notebook off the table, hoping her papers will scatter, hoping I will see the questions, commit them to memory so I can pass them on to Essence, Ronnie, Malachi, and Charles. But when Cynthia's notebook falls, no loose papers fly out and she picks it up before I can even bend over.

"Sorry," I say.

Cynthia gives me a half smile. "It's okay."

I sit back down, plot out another way. It comes sooner than I think it will. Cynthia raises her hand, asks to use the restroom. Mrs. Armstrong writes her a pass, and as soon as she is out of the door, I stand. Stretch. Survey the room, looking to see if anyone is watching me. I decide this is my only chance. I just have to walk over to her desk, take the notebook, open it, and get the questions. I look around one more time, then walk toward her desk, but decide to walk over to the bookshelf and pretend to be looking for something.

Can I really just open this girl's stuff?

I talk myself out of it, but then I think about how unfair it is that she gets to prepare and practice and no one else does. I know how these things go. The person who gets the head start usually wins the race. And Cynthia having those questions is Cynthia having a head start.

By the time I decide that I am going to do it—just walk over to her desk and read the questions, Cynthia is back and the bell is ringing, and I'm still plotting.

CHAPTER 69

I've been waiting for everyone to fall asleep, but Nikki has been on the phone with Ronnie for an hour. It's past midnight and if Mom knew either of us were still awake, she'd be fussing.

I finally hear Nikki's TV go on, which means she's off the phone and in bed. She goes to sleep to the sound of her TV. I usually end up going in her room in the middle of the night and turning it off because it's way too loud.

I wait for about fifteen minutes, and I think Nikki has fallen asleep, so I go into the hall, stand at the top of the stairs, and listen to see if Dad is up. I don't see any lights on, or hear any noise, so I go downstairs, make my way to his office.

He might have the questions. I'm sure he helped come up with them.

I get to the bottom of the steps and all I have to do is walk through the living room to get to Dad's office. But before I start walking, I see light seeping through the bottom of the door. Is he in there or did he just leave the light on?

I walk barefoot across the hardwood floor, step inches in front of his office door, put my hand on the knob, and the door opens without me even trying. "Maya?" Dad is standing in the doorway, startled but relieved. "I thought I heard something. Girl, you're going to give your ole man a heart attack."

"Sorry, I didn't mean to scare you."

Dad turns off the light to his office, closes the door. "What are you doing up so late?"

"Can't sleep."

I am hoping Dad will say something like, "Well, don't stay up too late," and go to his bedroom so I can sneak into his office, search for the questions. But instead Dad says, "Me neither." He walks into the living room, takes the remote control, and turns the TV on. "Want to join me?"

CHAPTER 70

"Girls! Girls!" It's ten o'clock on a Saturday morning. Why is my mother screaming? I turn over, pull my covers tight.

My door opens. "Maya, wake up." Now Mom is standing at the foot of my bed. "Nikki!" she yells. "We're in Maya's room. Come on. Get up."

Nikki stands in the doorway, wiping the sleep from her eyes. She yawns. "Mom."

"You have to open them together," Mom says. She hands both of us thick envelopes from Spelman.

I sit up and come from under the covers.

Nikki has her letter in hand before I can even get my envelope open. We read the letters silently. Both of us smile and scream and jump up and down.

"I'm so proud. So proud," Mom says. She and

Nikki start making plans—what to pack, what to buy there, how early we should get to Atlanta so we can get acclimated before classes start.

"So you're coming with me?" I ask Nikki.

"Yes. I'm going with you to Spelman," Nikki says.

I put my letter on my desk next to the brochures that Tony gave me. I stretch. Long. Reach for my ceiling and let out a yawning sigh. My eyes water. Maybe because of the yawn, maybe because when I look out the window and see Tony's shadow moving against his curtain, I think about how much I am going to miss him. Or maybe it's because Essence is in the guest room, probably pretending to be asleep, pretending she can't hear that her two closest friends are moving. And this time, the distance is a lot more than forty-five minutes away.

CHAPTER 71

"I want to see you," Tony says.

It is stormy outside and I don't feel like going anywhere.

"Are your parents home?"

"Yes. Yours?"

"Yep." Tony sighs. "Well, just come on a ride with me. We won't even get out of the car. I just want to see you."

"I'll be out in five," I say. I have on jeans and one of my dad's sweatshirts. I don't change, I just put on socks and shoes and run down the stairs. Mom is in her sewing room, Dad is in his office. "Dad, I'm going out with Tony. I won't be gone long."

"Okay."

Tony is waiting for me when I get outside. He has the car running, and when I get in, the car is already heated. He doesn't drive off just yet. We sit for a while, looking out at the rain. It crawls along the window, then disappears.

"Congratulations," Tony says.

"I wanted to be the one to tell you!"

"Kate," Tony says, smiling. "Nikki called her to tell her the good news." Tony takes my hand and traces his finger along my palm. "Do you know what I'm writing?" He presses into my skin three times.

"Do it again," I say.

He repeats the three marks, slowly.

"I?"

"Yes."

He keeps writing on my hand with his finger. "You can't look," he tells me.

I close my eyes. "That tickles." I pull my hand away and wipe it on my jeans.

Tony takes it back and keeps writing, but after three tries I can't guess what it says. So as he writes, he talks slowly, "I'm proud of you." He taps my hand as if to leave a period.

I take his hand and kiss it. "I'm going to miss you," I tell him.

He squeezes my hand, leans back in his seat.

We sit in the car, surrounded by rain and dark sky. The streetlights glisten against the fallen water, making the windows shimmer like a sequined dress.

CHAPTER 72

A week has gone by, and I haven't been able to get my hands on those interview questions, and the interviews are happening next week. Ronnie, Malachi, and Charles have made it as finalists. I know Cynthia has, too, which is why I am making the boys practice during lunch so they can be ready. Essence didn't make it as a finalist, so she's definitely going to beauty school. I talked her into taking business classes, too.

It's lunchtime and Essence and I are in The Lounge drilling them with questions we pulled from our college applications. "I'm sure it will be something similar," I tell them.

Mrs. Armstrong is at her desk eating her lunch and reading through a stack of essays from one of her English classes. She looks up from time to time and smiles.

Essence says, "Before we start, we need to talk about what you guys are going to wear." She looks at Ronnie and Malachi.

Ronnie says, "Why you not asking Charles what he's wearing?"

Charles laughs, and Essence says, "Because I don't ever have to worry about Charles looking put together. You and Malachi are the ones who think putting on a blazer with jeans and a button-up shirt is formal."

Malachi asks, "We have to dress formal for the interview?"

"No," I tell them. "But you shouldn't wear jeans. It's an interview."

"I'll help you guys with what to wear," Essence says.

"And I'll help all of you with what to say," I tell them.

For the next twenty minutes we role-play with each other and I ask them questions that I think the panel might ask.

A heavy knock pounds on the door, and Principal Green steps inside the classroom before Mrs. Armstrong can say, "Come in."

He is carrying a clipboard in his hand that has

papers and a pen tucked under the silver clasp. "Rachelle?" Mr. Greene calls Mrs. Armstrong by her first name. "Do you have a moment? I'd like to speak with you."

It's obviously not a question because Principal Green just keeps talking, not giving Mrs. Armstrong a chance to answer.

"What is this?" He holds up the worksheet on press releases that she gave us in class.

"You don't know what that is?" she asks.

"Don't be trite with me. Yeah, I know what it is, and I also know that some of your students have invited media here for the block party, which is something I didn't approve." Principal Green looks at me. "You can imagine my surprise when Channel 8 called to confirm the details." Principal Green looks over at us and says, "Uh, you all might want to leave—"

Mrs. Armstrong stands. "It's okay. They can stay."

Principal Green hesitates for a moment, then he says, "Do you know who sent the press release?"

"No," Mrs. Armstrong says.

"I find it interesting that posters were hanging around this school of people *you* were teaching to students, yet you didn't know who was behind that, and now you're telling me you don't know who sent the media a press release, when you're the one who taught them how to write one." Principal Green takes the top paper off his clipboard and tosses the paper toward the desk, and it blows to the floor. Neither of them bothers to pick it up. "Rachelle, you are a teacher. You are here to teach. Not lead political rallies or make a statement. These kids have a lot of learning to do, and the last thing they need is to be distracted by a movement. And furthermore, you don't have the authority to invite the press to this school for anything. We have administrators who handle public relations."

I can't believe Principal Green is talking to her this way. I want to say something. Defend her. But I know that it's not my place. Besides, Mrs. Armstrong is capable of handling her own. "Are you finished?" she asks.

"Actually I'm not. We wonder why kids aren't learning at Richmond, and then it all becomes clear. Teachers are using their prep time to chat with the students." He points toward us. "These kids are students. Not your friends. I need you to remember that." Principal Green turns to leave.

"I think you dropped something by accident," Mrs. Armstrong says, looking at the paper that fell to the floor. She arches an eyebrow and stares him down.

Who breaks it up when teachers fight?

Principal Green bends down and picks up the worksheet. "I apologize you all had to witness this, but it is important that you know the role of your teacher. I believe you can learn a lot from this."

"Excuse me, but I have something to say." Mrs. Armstrong is talking calmly, but her eyes are fire. "I was going to wait and ask if we could speak after school when our students aren't present. But since you'd like to use this as a learning opportunity for them, then let's do that."

Get him, Mrs. Armstrong. Get him.

"First of all, I didn't know students were inviting the press to the block party, but I must say I think that's a great idea—"

"The press is here enough as it is. There's an article on Richmond at least once a week," Principal Green says.

"And they never get the story right. Principal Green, you have a chance to let these kids tell their own stories. To let them speak for themselves," Mrs. Armstrong says. "To my knowledge, this block party is a celebration featuring alumni from this school who have gone on to accomplish great things. Seems like you'd be all for exploiting that."

No one is going to believe this has happened. I am so glad I have witnesses.

"I'm all for the block party," Principal Green

says. Then he looks at me. "However, this event is not academic. When the kids put on a science fair, we'll call the press." Principal Green puts his clipboard down on the desk. It slaps the table, echoes.

"Since when is critical thinking, innovation, and applying what you've learned in the classroom to the real world not academic? What is the point of education if it can't live outside the four walls of the classroom or break out of the multiple-choice boxes on a test? Our students have taken what they've learned in theory and put it into action. You should be proud of that."

I honestly think they've forgotten that we're in the classroom watching all this. This is just as awkward as when my parents argue in front of me. I try to distract myself, look somewhere else besides Mrs. Armstrong's burdened eyes. I look at the desk, notice pencil carvings and graffiti tags. My eyes scan the table. Principal Green's clipboard is sitting so close to the edge it might fall. I reach out to move it, but then pull back once I realize what's been sitting in front of me this whole time.

The questions.

CHAPTER 73

The school year is almost over. The closer it gets to summer, the more time I want to spend with Tony. Every weekend we do something together because we know that soon I'll be in the south and he'll be on the West Coast. He got accepted to Stanford.

I walk across the street to Tony's house and ring the doorbell. I hear footsteps, then the curtain at the front window moves. There is silence and then two clicks. The door opens. "Hello." It's Mr. Jacobs. He is in jeans and a blue T-shirt that is torn at the collar.

"Hi, uh, I'm—I'm here for Tony."

"He went to the store with his mom. He should be back soon." Mr. Jacobs opens the door wide. "You can come in and wait for him."

I am tempted to turn around and go back across

the street. I can wait at home. But Mr. Jacobs is smiling and already has the screen door open.

He goes into the kitchen, opens the fridge, and grabs a Coke. "Can I get you something to drink?"

"No, thank you." I sit on the sofa. I wish he had been watching TV so at least we could distract ourselves by making small talk about whatever was on. But instead, the house is silent. It was never, ever this quiet when Essence lived here.

Mr. Jacobs brings me a glass of water even though I didn't ask for anything. "Tony tells me you and Nikki are going to Spelman."

"Yes."

Mr. Jacobs drinks from his can of soda. "That's a long way from Oregon."

"Yes."

"Tony's going to Stanford." Mr. Jacobs sets his Coke down on a coaster. "He'll be soaking up all that sun."

"Yeah, and I'll be adjusting to Georgia's heat."

Why is it that talking about the weather is always a common denominator?

"Tony tells me you're really smart. Says you could go to any school you want."

I smile.

"That's good. You and your sister seem to have good heads on your shoulders. I should have you come talk to my students. They need all the inspiration they can get," he says. "They're not like you."

They're not like you.

The words hang in the room like thick smog.

I take a drink of water.

Outside two car doors slam shut and soon footsteps are on the porch. Just as the knob turns, Mr. Jacobs says, "Your parents must have done something right, that's for sure. You and your sister are the only kids I know from around here who got something good going for their lives." He takes a long drink from his can, stands, and opens the door for Mrs. Jacobs and Tony. "Keep up the good work," he tells me.

By the time I realize his words weren't really compliments—even though he probably thinks they were—by the time I remember that this isn't the first time a white person has told me I am not like the rest of them—my friends, cousins, neighbors—it is too late to say anything. And what would I say anyway?

Sometimes I am quick to stand up for myself, to let someone know that he needs to rethink what he just said. I can be that fire child Mom always says I am. But sometimes I am barely a flame. Sometimes I'm a coward.

CHAPTER 74

It's the end of May and our block party is getting off to a good start. This is the kickoff to the rest of our senior activities. Prom is in two weeks, then graduation. The street is blocked off to traffic so people can walk freely and not have to worry about cars.

After our block party, Jackson Avenue will open up for Last Thursday. We have a good representation from the local businesses. Most of them are giving out coupons to use at their shops.

I look around to see if any reporters are here, and so far none have showed up. It took a while for the sun to come out, but now that it's noon, the sky is glowing. I get the official program started by welcoming everyone and introducing the performers and speakers for the day.

The last person to speak is Mark Lewis, the doctor who has his master's from Brown. Mark takes the stage. At the end of his speech he says, "I am the man I am today not only because of the college I attended, not only because of my parents, but because of this community right here. Yes, I have a degree from Brown, and yes, I started a clinic. I guess that could be called success. But I believe I am successful because I try to live a life of integrity and because I practice empathy for others. I learned that here, right here at Richmond."

After Mark finishes his speech, Principal Green comes to the stage. "Ladies and gentlemen, this is Richmond High!" Principal Green says. "Now, allow me to do a little bragging. Miss Maya Younger, our student body president, and her twin, Nikki, have been accepted to Spelman College!" There are claps and whistles, and it feels so good to have all these people rooting for us.

Principal Green reads a list of Richmond seniors and which schools we will be attending. "And today, we are going to help make a dream come true for one more student," he says. "This student will get the Richmond High School Leadership and Community Involvement Scholarship," he says. "I would like Maya to do the honor of announcing our recipient."

Principal Green hands me an envelope. I know I

am supposed to say something like, “Everyone’s a winner,” or something else to those who won’t get the scholarship, but all I can do is rip open the envelope. From the corner of my eye I see Principal Green and one of the college advisers holding an oversize check. It’s turned so that the words are facing them and not the audience. I pull the paper out of the envelope, and I read exactly what it says. “It is my great pleasure to announce the recipient of the Richmond High School Leadership and Community Involvement Scholarship: Charles Hampton!”

CHAPTER 75

After the block party, Malachi and Ronnie congratulate Charles. They walk next to him and Devin, with Nikki, Essence, and me behind them. We meet up with Star, Tony, and Kate and walk Jackson Avenue going in and out of the shops using our coupons. All of us keep replaying the moment Charles took the stage, how his mom was crying and clapping and thanking God.

"And the look on Cynthia's face," Star says. "She just knew she won."

We all laugh, but then Charles looks at me and says, "Thank you, Maya," in a way that makes me know we are forever friends.

Vince and Bags are walking across the street with Cynthia and Tasha. Vince is dancing with a belly dancer and drawing a crowd. The more people laugh and point, the wilder he flops his arms and gyrates his body.

"Let's go in here," Essence says. "I'm hungry."

"You're willing to eat at Soul Food?" I laugh.

Essence holds up a coupon. "Girl, free food is good food."

The boys don't want to eat just yet. They keep walking and leave me, Essence, and Star with Nikki and Kate. The five of us go into Soul Food. Essence gets in line, and we grab a table at the window. I look out the window at the avenue, hoping to see the man who sold me the necklace. I want to thank him, tell him I know what it means. I look for him at the corner, but instead a local photographer is there selling her prints.

Z is here, too, pushing his cart down the sidewalk in front of Daily Blend. His cart is overflowing and piled so high I'm not sure if he can see where he is going. He bumps into Vince. He stumbles a bit but doesn't fall. Bags turns and starts yelling at Z. I can't make out what's being said, but I know it's nothing good. Vince and Bags are laughing at and taunting Z. Cynthia walks away from them, as if she wants no part of this. I see her squeeze herself through the crowd. People stop and watch the argument, and some of them even join in, yelling at Z, telling him he can't be here with his cart.

Z tries to move; he pushes his cart forward, but Vince and Bags won't budge and the street is so crowded, it's hard for Z to maneuver his way out. Now he is cursing and yelling, and everyone in Soul Food gets up from their tables and comes to the window to watch the drama.

Vince knocks Z's cart over and everything after that happens so fast, I'm not even sure what I'm seeing; all I know is Z and Vince are in each other's faces yelling and instead of people trying to break it up, people start arguing with each other, right in the middle of Jackson Avenue.

"There's no reason why he needs to bring that junk over here!" someone shouts. "If he doesn't want to act civilized he should stay home!"

I hear someone else say, "He has a right to walk this street just like everyone else!"

People are yelling. I can barely make out what anyone is saying, but I know there is arguing about who was in this community first.

And then I hear glass shatter. Someone has thrown a rock into the front window of Daily Blend. The mild chaos becomes total mayhem and everyone is running, trying to leave.

The owner of Soul Food locks her door, turns off the lights, tells us to come with her to the kitchen.

We hide in her dark pantry, sit on the floor. I can hear the sounds of more glass breaking.

There is one voice that stands out. It sounds like Vince, and he is saying, "This is our neighborhood, too!" I think back to the day when Devin got into it with Vince, to the words written on the wall—*This is our school, too*—and I wonder if all this, the buffet, the poster war, the assembly, has just been a joke to him and Bags. And I know I will never be able to say this for sure, but I think he said the n-word that day in the hall.

The store owner sits next to me on the floor. She is trembling. I take her hand. One of her cooks is on the phone with the police. When she hangs up, she says, "We just need to stay here, stay calm. Help is on the way."

CHAPTER 76

The next morning I wake up to the sound of the news. Nikki's TV must be up as loud as it can go. "There will be no school today at Richmond High," the reporter says.

I go into her room. Essence and Nikki are sitting on her bed. I get in, sit crossed-legged next to Nikki.

The news is replaying scenes from yesterday.

Of course they showed up to report about this.

Mom knocks on the door. Her eyes are still red from crying last night. When Nikki, Essence, and I walked in the door she couldn't stop hugging us, couldn't stop crying. "Good morning," she says. "Just wanted to check in. You girls okay?"

We say yes.

Mom stays in the room, watches the news with us. The camera scans over a block of Jackson Avenue. Daily Blend has the most damage. But other stores have broken windows, too.

A commercial comes on. I ask Mom, "Can I go over to Daily Blend and help clean up?"

"Maya, you are not leaving this house."

"But, Mom, look, the news is even saying that everything is under control."

"Maya, the answer is no."

"But—"

"Don't ask me again." Mom goes to her room.

I get up. Nikki is looking at me, and I know she knows what I'm thinking. "Let's go," she says.

The three of us get dressed and sneak out of the house.

The first place we stop is Daily Blend. Glass litters the streets. The sun reflects off it, giving us the illusion that we are walking on jewels. There are workers outside sweeping and a few people boarding up a window.

When Nikki and I approach them, one of them backs up, clinching her hammer. "We're here to help," I say. "We'd like to help you." I take the broom from one of the women who is sweeping, and I start cleaning the glass.

Just as I gather the last of the debris into the dustpan, a reporter comes up to me. "Mind if we speak to you for a moment?"

He gets the cameraman to come over, and he asks me, "So how does this feel to have the place you work at vandalized?"

"Oh, well, I don't work here," I explain. I don't plan on saying this next part. It just comes out. "I'm the student body president at Richmond High, and I wanted to come out here and help. And—and I'd, uh, I'd like to invite any other Richmond students—current or alumni—to come down and help. This is our home, and we have to take care of it."

The cameraman thanks me and goes into the store to speak with the owner. By the time he is out, Tony and Kate have come to help. Charles, Star, and a few students from journalism have come, too. I see a reporter talking with Charles, and one from a different station is talking to Star.

Within an hour, twenty students have arrived, and by hour three, I lose count. Jackson Avenue is full of Richmond volunteers putting our broken neighborhood back together.

CHAPTER 77

A cleansing is taking place. A stitching together of trust.

As we clean, we talk, and as we talk, we learn about one another.

We learn that Joyce, the owner of Soul Food, lost her father because of complications with diabetes. Her passion for healthy eating is her way of honoring her dad, of trying to prevent other families from having to lose someone that way.

I am hesitant to ask her, but I remember Mr. Washington saying how we need them and they need us, so I say, "Would you ever do a workshop or cooking lesson for students from Richmond? Could we maybe come here and learn about healthy eating and get some ideas for recipes?"

"I would love that," Joyce says. She gets excited and already has a name for it. "Summer Sunday Suppers. I close early on Sundays, but once a month I wouldn't mind staying after hours for a special class."

After leaving Soul Food, I walk over to meet Star and Charles at the art gallery across the street. I think, if Joyce wants to get involved with Richmond, maybe other businesses do too. By the end of the day, I have talked to as many owners or managers as I could. There were a few who weren't interested, but most were willing to hear me out.

The owner of the gallery offers the back wall of his space to exhibit the artwork of Richmond students. And Mandy from Daily Blend says she'd love to host a summer open mic series for teens. "Maybe we could do one once school starts," she says. "How does that sound?"

"Good," I tell her. "Sounds good."

SUMMER

CHAPTER 78

June.

The flowers are breathing again. The sun lingers, and days last and last. I have packed away winter, spring. Pushed their clothes to the back of my closet. But I keep my umbrella out.

Portland's rain is not gone forever. Even with the bluest of skies I know the rain is just behind the clouds. She will come again, then leave, and come.

She always does.

CHAPTER 79

It's the last day of school. Graduation is next week.

Nikki, Essence, and I are at my locker with Tony and Kate. We each finish cleaning out our lockers and meet up with Ronnie, Devin, and Malachi at the end of the hall so we can all walk together.

When we get to the crosswalk at Jackson Avenue, the red hand flashes, telling us not to walk. Essence looks up and points to the street sign. "Tony," she says. "Did Maya ever tell you that this street was named after my great-great-grandfather?"

"Really? No. I had no idea."

We all laugh.

Nikki pats Tony on his shoulder. "She's just playing with you."

"They don't believe me, Tony. But I'm telling you,

it is," Essence says. She says it so seriously, he looks like he doesn't know who to believe, but then Essence can't keep her laugh inside. It bursts through her cheeks, and Tony laughs, too.

I see Daily Blend across the street, tell Essence, "I know who would be able to tell us how Jackson Avenue got its name."

We all cross the street and go inside.

ACKNOWLEDGMENTS

For being the sankofa around my neck and encouraging me to "go back and get it," thank you, Cheryl Baker, Tokumbo Bodunde, David Ciminello, Ama Codjoe, Domonique Debnam, Cherise Frehner Mahoney, Nanya-Akuki Goodrich, Cydney Gray, Ellen Hagan, Pamela Hooten, Kori Johnson, Julie Just, Jonena Lindsley, Kamilah Moon, Khalil Murrell, Kia Smith, and Robyne Walker-Murphy. You all cheered me on by giving encouraging words or reading early drafts and spending many hours in coffee shops with me for writing dates and work sessions. Thank you.

To my sisters, Trisa and Dyan, I appreciate you so much for offering your homes to be my personal retreat during my visits to Portland. Thank you for hot tea and space to create freely.

A special thank-you to my team at Bloomsbury, Victoria Wells Arms and Laura Whitaker, for your patience and guidance.

Thank you, Portland, Brooklyn, and Harlem for being home at various times in my life. We have changed together. Your brownstones and bungalows, landscapes and skyscrapers, artists and activists, helped shape this story and continue to shape me.